END OF THE FOREST

ZORA FOX

Everyone knew to stay away from the wood at twilight. Maidens most of all.

Every young girl heard the stories whispered around the fire by her grandmother and great-grandmother. Countless young women had gone missing at the edge of the wood. In Selene, girls' thirteenth birthdays were a time for caution and dread and warnings, not celebration.

Mine was spent inside with my sister Lizzie. We snuck away from the watchful eyes of Mother and Grandmother and Great-grandmother to slurp rich hot chocolate from full mugs. I was against it at first, but Lizzie insisted. That was the only time I'd ever drunk chocolate. Lizzie had bartered some from a rich merchant's son.

"I'd like to see one of the forest creatures," she said that day, only half in jest.

"Don't say that," I hissed. "If you hear the call to buy, don't answer."

The forest creatures called to maidens at the edge of the wood, luring them deeper with the promise of delicious fruit and delicacies. Since none of the maidens who answered the call were seen again, everyone in Selene knew they must have been killed, if not by the forest creatures, then by the wild Fae. Collectively, the town called them goblin men. All were murderous.

Once, before that birthday, I had seen something through the trees—a wide, dark deer's eye and short, graceful antlers, but the face otherwise human, even beautiful. Chestnut hair curled around the horns, blending into the bark of the trees.

He saw me. I thought he might even have been watching me. I never told anyone but Lizzie, because Mother probably would have locked me in my room, repeating the rhyme I'd been taught as a child:

> *"We must not look at goblin men,*
> *We must not buy their fruits:*
> *Who knows upon what soil they fed*
> *Their hungry thirsty roots?"*

Even the boys in town played the skipping game to that song until they reached ten or so and realized they didn't have to fear for themselves.

Grandmother felt bitter about this, eyeing all men with distrust. She often told the tale about when her two best friends, Jeanie and Polly, were taken. They'd all been sixteen. She had fallen ill and so didn't go to the edge of town to gather berries with the others. She would have scoffed at my story of the fawn-boy, fear tinging the edges of her reaction.

Great-grandmother was so old now that she didn't often say much, and even when she did, her advice and comments conflicted.

My sighting through the trees was years ago. After declining to look after the Coopers' three children, Lizzie now worked as a bookbinder and I had become a gardening assistant for Mr. Pruett. Mother lamented Lizzie's chosen profession for two reasons: bookbinding required dangerous travel to northern cities to sell her wares and she thought it distracted Lizzie from finding a husband.

In a town woefully short of women, most saw marriage and children as their sworn duty. At twenty, Lizzie had already received three proposals and turned down everyone. Though just a year younger, I'd received none at all. I wasn't surprised. Lizzie sparkled and twirled through life with a romantic wildness that inspired children and terrified adults. I gardened quietly, trying to do right by my family and avoid the many dangers of being a woman in Selene. The quiet didn't bother me. It gave ample space for my imagination to supply the excitement that my real life lacked. While Lizzie rushed toward adventures, I spun them in my head. Perhaps I'd even write them down one day for her to bind into a book. A foolish thought. For who would read them?

❧

"WHAT ARE THE INGREDIENTS IN A SLEEPING CHARM?"

"Valerian root, lavender, clover ash..."

Lizzie grinned and pointed at me huddled in the dirt, pulling weeds. "I knew it! I knew something was missing."

"Are you reading the books again?" I asked. Then I frowned. "Who wrote a new book of charms?"

She waved a dirt-smudged hand. She'd rummaged through my patch of mint as though searching for answers there before she asked me the recipe. I wasn't a practitioner exactly, any more than the other citizens of Selene were, but I had a good memory for potions. One day—who knew?—one could keep me safe from the woods.

"That doesn't matter, especially now that I know that clover ash was missing. A faulty book, and now I still have to sell it." She sighed dramatically and perched herself on a garden bench.

"It will help Mother and me," I said, hoping to cheer her and also remind her that we couldn't afford to be so principled when it meant losing money. We were the only family in Selene made up entirely of women. It made some suspicious, as though we had struck a deal with the Fae King himself, who was rumored to rule on the other side of the barrier. Others saw us as weak and protectionless. All found us a little odd.

We were a little odd. That, I didn't mind.

"Fine, yes," she admitted, picking a nearby raspberry.

I widened my eyes at her in admonition, but then I smiled. We weren't supposed to take anything from the garden, though I'd longed to more than once. "Just don't let them see you," I whispered.

She flounced to her feet, happily munching the berry. "It's sour anyway. You wouldn't like it."

"I'm sure I would," I said mournfully.

"Yes," she laughed. She knew I would stop her from plucking another for me. "You would. Are you coming to the full moon dance tonight?"

"I didn't know there was going to be another one."

"It's secret, of course. We don't want terrible Eric to come— he's far too old—or for Mother to find out. It's in Jonathan's barn."

Going was a dangerous proposition. Full moons meant that maidens were more likely to disappear into the woods, taken behind the barrier into the Other Kingdom.

"We'll go together," Lizzie coaxed.

I sat back on my heels, rubbing my hands together to get the dirt off as I considered. "It's not a good idea," I mused.

"But it's a fun idea. You'll be twenty in two days and you never get out to experience the world." She nudged my shoulder.

"And you do too much." I leveled a look at her. "One day, something will happen." I hated to dampen her spirit, but I couldn't bear the thought of her disappearing too. There was no one I loved more in all the world. Just as no boy had noticed me, I'd noticed none of the boys in that way I read about in fairy tales. And I couldn't confide in Mother or Grandmother the way I could with Lizzie. I'd be perfectly content if we two lived together one day in a cozy cottage, near enough to Selene to see Mother and far enough to be safe from the goblin men of the song.

"Have you ever wondered why so many people follow the forest creatures in the first place?" Lizzie asked, looking thoughtful.

"Yes. It seems so foolish and obvious!" I'd wondered for a long time, but it was bad form in Selene even to reference the disappearances unless it was to reinforce caution. "If a forest creature calls and offers to sell enchanted fruit, why answer?"

"The fruit must be delicious." She shrugged, a rueful smile tugging at her lips, almost as if she wished she could see for herself.

The image of the deer-like face I'd seen in the brush that day flashed in my mind.

"Or maybe the men are too beautiful and Selene women would rather try their luck with them?"

"Lizzie!"

"Really, though. Are there any prospects here?"

I had to admit there weren't for me, but there were for Lizzie. "It doesn't matter. They don't go off to *marry* them. They... disappear."

Everyone knew that meant murder or mauling or something

even worse, but no one could cross safely into the Other Kingdom to find out, not even the grown men of the village. Legends told of a few men who had tried to save their lady loves. Once they crossed the threshold into the Other Kingdom, they never returned either. At least, not in one piece.

I shuddered.

"No need to be so serious. I'm only joking," Lizzie said. "A bit of adventure would be good for you, though. So how about that dance?"

"Full moons in summer are the worst," I protested. "Mother will notice we're gone."

"I'll say we have to run an errand in Shegle. I'll go with you. We can protect each other. You know I'd never let anything happen to you. If those goblin men call, I'll fight them off."

I smiled despite myself. Lizzie, beautiful Lizzie with her long blonde braid and green dress and earnest eyes, would certainly try to fight on my behalf if it came to it. I'd bet on her against any other girl in town, who mostly resembled me, at least in the level of caution I showed.

Feeling daring, I leaned backward to pick some clover and handed it to a delighted Lizzie. "We can fight them off together."

❧   2   ❧

Sleeping charms were harmless. Mother would wake without knowing we had been gone longer than she expected. This way, we could have our fun and not worry her. She had already been through so much.

I wore my finest pink dress. Lizzie said it showed off my freckles. She drew the warding symbols on me with a delicate golden brush. Even she wasn't cavalier about either the brush or the symbols whenever she went out at night. That golden brush was worth half of everything else in the house, and none of us would part with it. Great-grandmother no longer told the full story of how she had gotten it, and the tale had changed over time anyway. One version said she'd received it from a beautiful young man she'd met in her youth who swore it had powers against the Fae, another claimed she'd gone on an adventure and had learned the secrets to making them herself, and in another she said she found it in the ruins of her family's home after it had burned in a fire with a note attached, saying, "For warding."

Generations of women in our family had kept it secret, used it when magical dangers were high, and none of us had ever gone missing.

A book with symbols of protection accompanied the brush. Handwritten notes darkened the margins. By now, Lizzie and I had our own preferences and opinions about which symbols to use. I trusted her judgment as she drew a curling script around my shoulder. It wasn't unusual to see young women in Selene painted with charms and wards, but our symbols were unique and we owned the only gold brush and paint.

We tiptoed out of our little house, past the curl of smoke in the crackling fireplace, lit despite the warmth of the day. Hinges creaked as we opened the door and shut it softly behind us. The day's heat had settled like a fur blanket over the village, cozy now, with little cool breezes tickling up our legs. The air smelled like stars and caramelly wood. I fought back a tremble at how *good* everything felt.

At this time of night, I was usually curled up reading a book. Lizzie sometimes went out for work or play, but I didn't.

Nights were dangerous. Nights were never for a young woman alone. But I wasn't alone. I would never be alone with Lizzie beside me. I beamed across to my older sister. She stood tall and indomitable, pale against the backdrop of black trees and navy sky.

This dance could be enjoyable after all.

The sugary woods odor gave way to the richness of cooked bread. My mouth immediately watered. I detected cherries and baked dough in a combination that could only mean my favorite dessert was in that barn.

Low light streamed through the slats, illuminating little puffs of dust escaping under the door. Horses whinnied within. Already, I could tell that more of the village had turned up to this illicit dance than I expected. Was everyone a rule-breaker but me?

Simultaneously comforted and disconcerted, I took Lizzie's hand as we slipped inside.

Garlands of stinging nettles wound together with blood-red string draped over the entire ceiling, creating a sort of perilous wilderness. That, along with colorful masks hung on the stable walls and stacked on tables, gave me the sense I'd walked into the Other Kingdom. About thirty people danced in the center of the barn, under the nettles, arms outstretched in an ecstasy of abandon. Music encompassed little more than vibrations and the soft whine of strings. The wildness of it all balled my stomach.

Something hard and thin pressed into my hands. A mask.

"Put it on!" Lizzie cried, donning her own disguise, which made her look like a wicked cat.

Mine was a large-eyed creature with sharp teeth and red lips that still managed to look somewhat alluring. I grimaced at it.

Lizzie laughed, the sound muffled. She already moved to the music, taken by the spirit of the place.

Did I want to be taken too? Well, I certainly didn't want to spend every night of my life reading at home, afraid of what might happen if I took the slightest risk. There was a large group of us here. The forest creatures couldn't get us. I was safe.

Sighing, I put on the mask. That simple action loosened my inhibitions. I recognized almost everyone there, but the disguises had changed some of them so much I could hardly tell they were themselves. There was Anders the delivery boy, and John the butcher's assistant, and Harriet the sheriff's daughter.

They invited me in as though they didn't ignore me in the street for being one of the "odd ones." So I let the music take me, its beat reverberating through my feet and into my very core. I couldn't even see where the music was coming from. Quiet like the others, I moved in time with the thumping, letting the worries of my day, my week, my month melt away into nothing but sensation. Here, it didn't matter who I was or that I always avoided the edge of the woods. It didn't matter that no one in town fancied me or that Mother constantly feared for me or that we were poor and hungry. None of it mattered. I was embraced by everyone in this wild-liminal space. I got drunk off everything, shedding layers of my carefully sheltered self. We drew each other close, everyone, moving to the music and feeling the bodies around us and the greenery above us. I longed to stay in this place. Its evanescence made it sweeter, more desperate, more secret. A false reality, an Other Kingdom.

When the vibrations slowed and I caught my breath, I found myself at the edge of the group. I'd forgotten about the cherry hand-pie I'd smelled before we entered. Raising my head, trying to shake off my daze, I searched for Lizzie. Was she still among the dancers?

It had to be getting late. With that thought, my trance was officially broken. I took off the mask to get a better view. I couldn't see Lizzie, but that didn't mean she wasn't somewhere in the hushed maelstrom of bodies. Had I really been part of that myself just moments ago? I chastised myself even while I yearned to rejoin them. But I couldn't. Not now. Sanity had returned, and with it, the realization that I was starving for cherry pastry and that it was now far too late for young women, accompanied or not, to be out near the woods.

I found the hand-pies first, moaning as the tart sweetness hit my tongue. Grandmother only made hand-pies on Saint Victor's Day. There was such a pile of them. Would they go to waste if they weren't eaten at this dance? The idea scandalized me so I took two more.

Still, Lizzie did not appear. Concern began to gnaw at me.

I threaded my way back through the dancers, hearing the call of subterranean desires once again, but this time I kept my head about me.

"Lizzie," I called in a scream-whisper.

Only heads of foxes, goblins, birds turned to heed my call.

"Lizzie!"

I knew I couldn't be too loud or the neighbors would wake and find us here. Consciousness surfaced in a dozen eyes to find me a stranger here, an uninvited guest. Inside, I soured a little but I soldiered on. Lizzie had to be here. No one said where she had gone.

My heart beat faster when I reached the opposite end of the barn. A glossy-eyed horse watched me over the stall door, but Lizzie was nowhere. I struggled to calm myself. She frequently made impulsive decisions but that didn't mean she'd traipsed into the woods to answer the call of a forest creature. She hadn't been taken.

But it was a full moon in summer. The barn lay close to the edge of the barrier where, even in daylight, peril haunted the steps of any who drew near the thick trees. And Lizzie was gone.

I tried to stifle my panic, but it rose to my throat. Grabbing the arm of the nearest dancer, I wrenched them toward me. The blank eyes of a squirrel met my gaze. "Did you see where Lizzie went?" I asked.

The person merely canted their head, animal-like.

"Did you?" I prompted, trying to shake them out of their haze.

"Laura? Stop bothering people."

I whirled at the sound of the laughing voice. By the back door of the barn stood Lizzie with her red-eyed cat mask. Air gusted from my lungs. I swept toward her.

"Where were you?" I demanded.

"There was no need to be so worried." I sensed her smile fade behind the mask when I didn't thaw. She took my hands, at once an invitation and apology. "I'm sorry I took you out of the fun. I was just behind the barn there," she whispered. "I wouldn't have gone if I knew you would be afraid for me. It was only a moment."

Over her shoulder, I saw another masked figure enter the back way. Although the exaggerated face of a wolf obscured his features, I recognized James, who had recently inherited his father's bakery. His sulking mouth had never appealed to me, but Lizzie sometimes spoke to him despite having no money for his baked treats. Perhaps the hand-pies had come from him.

I turned pleading eyes to my sister. "Please don't run off like that."

"Run off?" she laughed. "I was right here."

"Jeanie and Polly," I murmured, knowing she would understand.

She bent even closer, speaking muffled into my ear. "But I would fight, remember?" She straightened. "I will stay in here if it will make you happy."

But I was finished with this party. My mind rebelled against losing myself as I had before. In losing myself, I had almost lost Lizzie, which would have been unforgiveable. I trusted her to love me, but not always to keep herself safe. I was her voice of caution, her anchor, and I'd let that role slip.

"Can we leave? It's getting late."

Lizzie pulled off her mask. Her face was flushed. Blonde hairs floated wild around her face and her gaze was serious. "Anything for you."

I'd been afraid she would refuse, and it was far too dangerous to walk home alone in the darkness. With Lizzie, I'd be safer. "Then let's go."

"Did you enjoy yourself, though?" she pressed as we wound our way back to the front entrance.

"For a while," I admitted, not sure how else to respond. I returned my mask to the pile. No one seemed to mind our leaving. The unreality of the dancers persisted in their quiet, rhythmic movements. Even James didn't inquire after us. I cast one more look at the enchanted ceiling, stood still enough to feel the vibrations once more, and then the two of us left, plunged into solid darkness.

SAFE AT HOME, I TOOK OUT PEN AND INK IN FRONT OF THE fire. In the chair near where I sat on the floor, Great-grandmother stirred pleasantly in her sleep. Stirred by residual desires, I resolved to write them in a story. I'd already been working on a fairy tale, but now I started something new about a girl and her sister on a perilous, romantic adventure to the Other Kingdom. The truth about that place had been lost to legend, leaving me to fill it in as colorfully as I wished. Odd incidents and deaths sometimes trickled out from the barrier, but nothing apart from the vanished maidens held any consistency in our lives.

My neck ached from craning it down at the paper so long. Characters and incidents took shape beneath my pen. Orange fireglow flickered over the floor.

A hand touched my back. "You should go to bed before the sun rises," Lizzie said quietly, standing above me in her nightdress.

I hadn't yet changed into my nightclothes. "The sun...?" At first, I couldn't register her words. Had I been writing that long?

"You must be exhausted from all the excitement." She glanced down at the stack of paper.

I looked down guiltily. Paper and ink were luxuries, but I

would forgo meat if it meant an outlet for my longings, an expansion of my limited life.

"Is that the Tale of Orlando and Genevieve?" She snatched the pile from the floor. I was too late to stop her. Eyes roving over my small, spiky handwriting, she smiled.

I waited, tense, for her reaction. I'd never written anything quite like this story before. No one but Lizzie would ever be allowed to read it. Mother would faint if she found out what lurked in my carefully protected heart.

"No," she purred. "This is different. It's absolutely delicious!"

I stood to face her, looking at the pages alongside her as she held them out. Great-grandmother's hand moved on the threadbare armrest of the chair.

"I could speak to the bookbinder for you—"

"No," I cut her off. No one in Selene wanted to hear from a woman, much less one from our family. Besides, I couldn't bear the embarrassment of another soul reading it. I guarded my pages as jealously as the gold brush.

Lizzie softened, drawing me in. "I think it's lovely. One day, you should publish. But if you don't want to, then just write it for me. I could devour this for days!"

A swell of emotion choked me as I looked into my sister's face. That story had been born of dark longings, something intimate that showed my soul naked, but she didn't laugh or dismiss me for it. She never would. She loved me and I loved her.

I squeezed her sideways in a hug. Perhaps it was too late to be awake. I had work to do in the morning.

"Let's get you to bed," she soothed, guiding me toward the room we shared. She held me in the few hours before sunrise, as protective of my heart as I tried always to protect her.

❀   3   ❀

Mother stirred sugar into her tea the next morning. Her eyes looked shadowed. "Would Mr. Pruett let you bring home some dandelions, Laura?" she asked. Grandmother scoffed bubbles into her drink.

"I don't know," I admitted. I felt shadowy too after getting so little sleep the night before. "Why?"

"The neighbors reported some noises last night."

I met Lizzie's eyes across the little table. Sometimes disconcerting noises did come from the woods, especially on full moon nights, but I suspected the sounds were due to something else this time. "You want to hang them over the door?" I asked Mother.

"Maybe I can find some wild ones instead," she said staunchly. "Don't bother Mr. Pruett."

"I'll ask him."

"He wouldn't give the child a weed if she asked," Grandmother grumbled.

"Lilac," Great-grandmother chided, patting Grandmother's arm with her veiny hand, "we don't want weeds here."

"I didn't say I want weeds," said Mother.

"A dandelion is a weed," Grandmother replied.

"Just something for a little extra protection. I sense dark things moving about." Mother's eyes hooded. She looked older than her years.

"Laura and I can whip up a foolproof protection charm for you, can't we?" Lizzie winked at me.

Mother frowned, though the lines around her eyes grew less pronounced. "Don't tease, Lizzie."

"I'm not. Laura has a knack for these things. I bet I could walk through the forest naked at sunset and still return home next morning."

I kicked her leg under the table as Mother gasped. "Have you not heard a word I've tried to teach you?" Mother snapped. "Don't tempt the darkness or it will take you. *Who knows upon what soil they fed...?*"

"*Their hungry thirsty roots,*" Lizzie finished, setting her napkin on the tabletop with an air of irritated finality.

"I'll get dandelions for you, Mother," I said.

"Just not from Mr. Pruett," Grandmother mumbled, nibbling at her scone.

"He's a just man," Mother said, settling back in her chair, though she still looked sidelong at Lizzie, who was rising to leave.

"Yes, Laura will take care of everyone." Lizzie stood imperious now, a caged creature longing for freedom. "I have a long day at the binders today. Don't expect me back until just before dark," she announced.

"Make sure someone walks you home," said Mother.

"I can take care of myself."

"That doesn't mean you can't be careful!"

I'd heard this argument a thousand times. Mother already looked desperate with worry over her oldest daughter.

"Let her go," squeaked Great-grandmother. "She's a capable girl."

Lizzie looked triumphant.

"I will expect you back no later than sunset," Mother said pointedly.

Lizzie gave Mother a swift kiss on the cheek. "You know I don't want to worry you," she said in her ear. "I'll be back in time."

"Goodbye!" I called as she left. She waved at me on her way out the door. The memory of the barn door made me bite my lip. I wanted to trust her to stay out of trouble, but I could worry as well as Mother sometimes.

❦

I FOUND DANDELIONS GROWING WILD IN A FIELD ADJACENT TO James' bakery. Almost guiltily, I plucked some, knowing that other families in the village liked to make them into wine or seasoning. I only knew of one other family who dabbled in charms and wards as much as we did, and they were far better off than we were, so I didn't worry about them.

After tying four bunches together with red string like I'd seen at the dance, I hung them on the lintel of our front door, draped like a rich woman's finery. The bright yellow looked lovely against the red door, and Mother's heart would be put at ease.

The long day attending to Mr. Pruett's garden left my hands permanently soiled. Tiny lacerations covered my fingers and my short nails were rimmed in black.

Calloused hands wouldn't get a man, some people in the village said, but that had been true before I'd begun my gardening work. I liked being close to the land, snuffing up the rich soil smell and learning the properties of different plants. Since I was bound to be a spinster anyway at this rate, I might as well enjoy it. One day, perhaps, I could have my own garden and grow exactly what I liked—not only things like clover and lavender but poppies and radishes and sweet carrots. Lizzie and I would live together in a cottage. I'd already chosen it, though now it was occupied by the sheriff's family of six. I'd written stories about it in my mind, dreaming away nights snuggled next to Lizzie.

Grandmother emerged from the house. She flinched away from the bunch of dandelions hanging low enough to brush her forehead. "What—?" Her initial annoyance melted into a sardonic smirk. "Well done, girl. Your mother will be pleased. I hope you took them from that garden."

I smiled noncommittally. I would never steal.

She trundled a small woven rug into the light, hitting it with a beater. The sinking light cast strong beams across the back of her gray head. Flying dust looked like sparkles.

"Is Lizzie back yet?" I asked.

Grandmother paused to eye the horizon. Dark trees rose only a few meters from our front doorstep, deep shade dwelling underneath like inky water. "She still has a little time." But her voice was small. I knew she was thinking about her vanished friends, even after all this while.

My chest felt a little tighter, as it always did when I didn't know where Lizzie was. I shook off the feeling and hurried inside, trying to outrun my worry with work. I turned our mattress and rearranged jars of herbs in the kitchen. I added kindling to the metal pail and swept the floor in front of the hearth where cinders had flown.

When Lizzie still didn't appear, I gravitated toward the front door again. The sky looked blue as deep water with charcoal clouds streaked across it.

"Laura!"

I squinted toward the shed, where the sharp voice had come from.

"Laura, come here!" Lizzie sounded insistent but not alarmed, so I picked up my skirts and ran to our little outbuilding. My sister stood on the opposite side from the house, rosy-cheeked, with her hands behind her back. She seemed far too nonchalant for a young woman returning at twilight.

"What are you doing?" I demanded. "Come inside!"

"First," she said coyly, "I have something for you."

"What are you talking about?" My attention darted to the hands she held behind her back. My anger and distress started to subside. This was what Lizzie was so good at, how she could always win us back.

"It's your birthday tomorrow, so I thought I'd get you this." She held out an enormous leather-bound book with gilt lettering. I'd never seen something so fine.

Confused, I took it from her. The actual pages of the book were rather thin but the brown cover was large enough to hug to my chest like a breastplate. On the front it said "Tales of Orlando and Genevieve by Laura of Selene".

I gasped and shoved the book back at Lizzie. "I can't take this. How much did you pay for it?" Some of my horror was linked to how fervently I longed for that book. I ached with wanting it, a thing I'd never seen until that moment. But there was no way I could own such a thing. Months of work wouldn't afford it.

"It doesn't matter. It's all taken care of," she said, beaming as she handed it back to me. "I want you to have it. I've always loved your stories."

"I need to know how you got the money to pay for this." No matter how hard I thought, nothing made sense.

She brought her blonde braid over her shoulder. "I agreed to marry James last night."

I almost dropped the book. "What? But he didn't even talk to you before we left." That couldn't be right. Lizzie and I would live in the sheriff's cottage with my little garden, growing into stooped old women together.

"He's proposed a few times and I said no," she admitted airily. I knew that tone. She was putting on a mask now as surely as the wicked cat from the night before. "But something you said struck me. You said that we should do all we can to take care of Mother and Grandmother, all of us. James agreed to let me stay on as a bookbinding assistant, so I can still travel sometimes to sell books. His bakery sells all the bread in town, so none of us will go hungry. He has more than enough. I can send some home to you every week."

Tears blurred my vision. She didn't love James. Only the truest love would have convinced me to let go of Lizzie, of our dream. "You can't do this," I croaked. "You don't have to. We're getting along fine with both of our jobs..." With winter coming, my gardening work would all but end. Mr. Pruett was a fine employer, but he wouldn't hand out charity once I'd completed my work for the season. I clamped my mouth shut.

Lizzie regarded me knowingly. Her eyes lowered to the book in my grip. "I wanted to do something nice for you, for all the family. This won't be the end for us," she said, gripping my shoulders gently. "I'll come over as often as I can. Maybe I can even host suppers at our home." She hiccupped on the word *our*, though she laughed it off.

I glared knowingly back.

"And look what I could give you for your birthday!"

"It's too much," I whispered, my last feeble attempt to dissuade her. "I don't want it."

Lizzie looked as though I'd cursed her. Pain and anger shot

through her look. "Well, I'm marrying James with or without your blessing. Burn the book if you hate it so much."

Before I could open my mouth to protest, to say I loved the gift but would not accept her sacrifice, she'd stormed away.

In the wrong direction.

"I'm sorry," I said, chasing after her.

The sky looked a shade lighter than black now. Night had truly fallen. It was no time to be out, with or without Lizzie.

"Come back!" I cried. "I'm sorry." I wanted to say more than that, but if an apology would get her inside the house, I'd get on my knees.

My steps were clumsy since I clutched the book to my chest.

Lizzie was being childish. She would return. I had to get back to safety myself.

Casting one last look toward the edge of the forest, I turned reluctantly back to the house. Guilt tugged at my sternum. She had bought me the loveliest birthday present I'd ever received, and I criticized her for the sacrifice it took for her to get it. How long would she sulk or cry or whatever she was doing? She knew any delay would kill me.

I tried to hide the book as I went inside. Our house was tiny, and Mother sat by Great-grandmother in front of the cold hearth. It was a warm night, but Great-grandmother still held a shabby yellow blanket over her legs.

Mother surely saw what I held, but, out of character, didn't ask any questions about it. Instead, she said, "I heard Lizzie's voice. Is she home too?"

I couldn't answer. My throat had gone tight. No, she wasn't home, and it was all my fault. Hopefully she wouldn't put herself in danger for many more minutes. As soon as she walked in, I would apologize and she would declare her choice to marry James and we could find a way to be happy again.

Back in the room I shared with my sister, I angled the leather cover to look again at the title. It was the most beautiful object I'd ever beheld, and it had my name. The gold script struck me. Lizzie must have used the golden brush. My lips twitched, not quite a smile or frown. It felt good to have someone willing to break the rules for me.

I would wait five more minutes. That was all. And then...

What would I do?

Genevieve would storm out to save Orlando, and vice versa. They wouldn't hesitate. They would have reckless courage, even if it meant running straight into danger.

Heartbeats drew me on from one second to the next. And the next. And still, no Lizzie.

That she was gone was my fault and, like it or not, I had to do something about it. I'd given up the search too quickly the first time. I would take a light... But the very thought made me short of breath. Wouldn't it be better to organize a search with other people? But then I'd have to reveal Lizzie's secret and the reason she didn't come straight home.

No, I had to go alone. I would be quick. I would go armed, with a light.

I dropped a little oil into the lantern on the stand by our bed, gripped the round metal handle, and shoved a paring knife into the belt of my dress. Lifting the book again—I couldn't leave it around for Mother to find, and besides, I could use it as an extra weapon if I had to—I waited until Mother's back was turned and went out.

The very air crackled with night dangers and magic. Those few minutes inside had deepened the darkness. Around me, a pool of yellow light brought everything into ghostly reality. I moved as swiftly as my dress and book and lantern would allow, skirting the edge of the woods. Far enough from the house not to be overheard, I called out to Lizzie once more. A bird tweeted somewhere in answer. Straining to listen, I heard nothing but the faraway sounds of someone cooking, a wagon being set in its resting place, and... music.

"Lizzie?" I cried, swinging my lantern toward the sound.

Tinkling bells and pipes and faint drums played on the edge of hearing.

"Lizzie?" She didn't answer, so I hurried forward again. She couldn't be far. Maybe she had followed the music too.

As it grew loud enough to make out a swirling tune, I realized the sound didn't come from Jonathan's barn or from the village at all. It came from the woods.

My arm shook as it held the lantern aloft. Trunks rose only a few steps in front of me, the space beneath lost in pathless darkness. I didn't know how far in the barrier was. Could I risk a couple steps inside the shelter of the trees?

I would fight them off for you.

What if Lizzie were in trouble? I couldn't stand here, close enough to do something but too cowardly to take action.

The strain of the decision racked my body.

Smells of something warm and sour-sweet rose above the scent of oil and tree sap. The music grew louder, an odd collection not quite of notes but a feeling.

I clutched the book, feeling its heaviness, and thought of the knife at my waist. Planting my feet and drawing in breaths of star-scented air, I plunged in to find my sister.

❄   4   ❄

Roots gnarled around my feet like snakes, the ground bumpy and uneven. Trees rose like an army on either side of me. Ahead, my lantern washed the dark trunks white. Breeze-blown branches stretched overhead, catching me by surprise every time.

"Lizzie?" I tried again, but my voice barely rose above the hush of leaves and eddying music. I adjusted the book in my grip. When I saw my sister again, I would thank her soundly for the gift, beg her forgiveness, and run home.

She must be with the music. It prickled across my skin with wild and tender notes in combinations that reminded me of feasts and rain and hoped-for kisses. Lizzie must have wandered after the sound as I was doing now.

Orange light glowed faintly from within a particularly dense copse of trees. Perhaps James and the others had raised the level of excitement and risk in their dancing and chose to host it here.

Cautiously, I stepped forward. The bones in my hand ached from holding so tightly to the lantern. Its shine met the edge of warmer light emanating from the trees. I hadn't imagined the sour-sweet smell or the cultured unruliness of the music. They surrounded me now. Behind a line of trees—almost a wall created of bark—was a hollow open to the forest on one side. Trampled grasses marked its boundary. Flowers sprang from everywhere, not placed like decoration but riotous like a field ablaze with spring growth. Tiny flames, perhaps candles, peeked out from between leaves everywhere I looked. On the ground lay dishes heaped with food and rustic goblets filled with drink. Plump cherries, down-cheeked peaches, full pomegranates, and thick sprigs of barberries stacked together or hung in baskets. All was fire and wine and flowers.

And the creatures, the creatures that inhabited this world of reckless beauty! They had a stealthy carelessness to their movements, lounging amid all this plenty. Together or alone, their attitudes were sensuous. Several had the legs of a deer. Others had fur on their faces or feathers like the finest bird. Some had human faces with tangled hair, and one had liquid eyes and a set of fine antlers.

I knew immediately that he had looked at me once, through the trees. His look of innocence was belied by the fox-fur females draped over him, gently caressing his chest and arms. He beckoned me with his eyes, a half-smile playing on his lips, still mostly human.

Heart slowing, I approached. Before him was a brass ewer and a tray of melon. I wasn't sure where to sit.

He wasn't the only one who seemed pleased to see me. The others, even the fox-fur women, looked at me with interest.

"Welcome, human girl," purred one of the beautiful creatures. I wasn't sure which one. I wanted to touch them all, to drink their wine and hear their voices.

"Try it," said the fawn-boy who had watched me that day. He saw I'd been looking at the green melon on the plate. Never before had I seen so much food wantonly set out at once. Some of the fruits I'd only seen pictures of, never tasted.

"I can't." Somewhere deep inside, I knew I didn't want to set down the large book I held, though I couldn't remember why.

"Come lie with us. We'll feed it to you." His voice was reedy, but not unpleasant. It was like the sound a squirrel makes in a tree or a bear makes as he snuffs the water in search of fish. It sounded like autumn.

One of the fox-girls giggled and plucked a piece of green fruit from the tray with her fingers. She pushed it with a fingertip into the mouth of the tousled fawn-boy.

I yearned to eat it. I clumsily lowered myself so I sat on my heels.

"Come closer, human girl," coaxed an elegant moss woman on my left. She tugged on the collar of my dress and I stumbled sideways. My hip hit the ground, crushing a rush of foxglove beneath me.

"Let me have her," said a male voice, yanking me in the other direction.

Upright again, I turned questioning eyes to the fawn-boy. He hadn't fed me the melon yet, but he held some glistening in his hand. I leaned forward to get it. He laughed when I failed.

"She can have these grapes, sugar-sweet and icy-cold," said a crackly new voice. A birch would have that voice if it could speak.

Something cold as snow pressed against my lips. I opened my mouth but was pulled sideways before I could eat. I fell to the ground, harder this time. The glass of my lantern shattered into stardust and oil leaked out like blood on the ground. The flame flickered and died.

Claws caught me. Fingers clutched at me. I couldn't see the fawn-boy anymore. My dress ripped from the neck and hung over one shoulder. The music had grown wilder. Wine splashed over my hair. I licked my lips to drink the sharp-smooth flavor but got none.

Madness threatened me. I had to get some food, some drink, some of the plenty around me. I stretched my free hand forward—the other still gripped the book—and felt for the edge of the tray.

A hand closed over mine.

Through the chaos of fur and feathers and claws, I saw the fawn-boy regarding me as calmly as he did the first time. His deep brown eyes steadied me. He reached forward, the melon still in his hand. Relief filled me as I leaned to meet him.

Bitter coin spray hit me in the face. Snarls and shrieks erupted. Many hands let go of me.

The fawn-boy lay slumped, black-red blood glugging from his severed neck. I screamed, hand flying to my mouth. Nausea swooped in my gut. What had just happened?

I swiveled to look around me, and the scene was like a dream made real. Forest creatures ran in terror, upending bowls of fruit in their flight. Candle flames waved. Hanging baskets teetered. I felt as though I'd just woken up, having found myself in a strange bed with no memory of how I'd gotten there. Disoriented and horrified, I stumbled to my feet. The lantern lay in pieces. Even in the dark, I had to escape whoever—*whatever*—had done this to the fawn-boy. Only the two of us were left, myself and the corpse.

I blinked frightened tears away and tried to will my legs to run. They moved creakily, like an ungreased puppet, but I sped away from the hollow as fast as I could go.

Is this what happened to the maidens of Selene? Were they ruthlessly beheaded or lured into magical places only to get hopelessly lost in the woods?

And where was Lizzie?

At the thought of my sister, I cursed myself. How could she

not have been the very first thing on my mind? Surely, she'd encountered foul play here in the forest, but where?

I couldn't call out, not while I was being pursued.

I rubbed more tears out of my eyes. When I could see well enough to continue, an enormous black horse stood in front of me. Or at least it looked black in the darkness. The candle flames from the hollow and the nearly full moon illuminated not only the huge feathered horse but also its rider—a large, dark-haired man with disdainful eyes and features more beautiful than any I'd seen on a mortal human. With one hand, he insolently held the reins. With the other, he held a long, bloody knife.

I froze.

"Take her," came his rich voice.

Before I could turn to see who he was talking to, a bag dropped over my head, the book was ripped from my hands, and I was swept away into the night.

Cool wind whipped across my face in the speed of my riding. Behind me, a strong body pressed against my back, holding me in place. Though I wasn't bound, apart from the bag over my head, I didn't sense that I would fall. I smelled the horse beneath me and felt the heavy rocking of its gallop, but somehow the hooves made barely a sound in the underbrush. Horror had initially ripped away my voice, but I started to catch my breath.

There was more than one rider. That much was clear. Who were these people? Were they more forest creatures, at war with each other or simply savage enough to kill at random? The man I'd seen, if he could be called a man, didn't look like the pretty beings in the hollow. His beauty was unearthly, hard and unyielding, like a god of war.

They'd taken my book. That, somehow, was one of the most painful parts of all this. If they took me to Lizzie, I'd be grateful, despite the terrifying circumstances.

My experience in the hollow felt hazy, but flashes of memory returned as I rode. Those were the goblin men, the ones who offered fruit to maidens who were never seen again. My face felt sticky with wine and juice and blood, but I couldn't remember eating anything. Wind cooled my bare shoulder. When had my dress ripped?

A complicated net of emotions—shame hot among them— reared up in me. I'd wanted the fruit. That much I remembered. Had I not been warned over and over again as a child? Had I not been taught the song?

The horses seemed to be slowing, so I perked up my senses. We weren't in the village. Of course not. Why would we be? Instead, I felt forest coolness around us and smelled spicy woodsmoke. Beyond that, there was nothing but nighttime insects calling to each other. Not a breath or word from my sister.

My captors didn't speak a word either as they quietly dismounted and led me up a flight of hard stairs, then down a straightaway, and then down another, narrower set of steps. What would they do to me once we arrived? I didn't want to think. No young woman ever reappeared in Selene after being taken to the Other Kingdom.

Lizzie's promise to fight sounded flimsier now. Carefully, I felt for the paring knife at my belt but found nothing. The man on the horse had taken it, no doubt, in the flurry of my capture. And what could it have done against his long, bloody one anyway?

The helplessness of my situation almost overwhelmed me. I wasn't used to danger. I couldn't stare at a challenge this insurmountable and prevail. But now, what choice did I have? Either I could die quietly or I could try to get some answers first.

The rough hand gripping my shoulder halted. The hushed shuffle of several other feet stopped too.

Light returned in a burst that made me wince as the bag was whisked from my head. Flyaways from my braid tickled my cheeks and eyes and stuck to my lips. My vision focused on a man, the same one who had ridden the black horse. He blocked my view of the rest of the room. Finely articulated dark leather, cut like some type of armor, covered his broad chest and shoulders, emphasizing the muscles there. At his hip hung a scabbard where he must have kept the bloody knife. He was tall, much taller than I was. Dark hair, almost black, fell around his face. His cut jaw and intense eyes seemingly lit from within suggested the vigor of youth, but he had the unhurried confidence of someone older. I couldn't begin to guess his age.

With his blood-speckled hands and golden stare, he emanated power.

"What were you doing in the forest, foolish girl?" he snapped, his voice deep and commanding.

My brows lowered. "I was looking for my sister. Do you have her too?"

"We don't have time to track down all the humans who wander into the woods."

Heat flushed my face. "Do you know where she is?"

"Did you hear what I said? No. She's gone by now, in all prob-ability."

"Gone?" I breathed. My hands balled into fists. Everything I had carried with me to help Lizzie was gone too. I had nothing left and now I was at the mercy of this person.

"You could thank me," he said, his low voice rumbling with irritation.

My head snapped up. "Thank you? For what?"

"For saving you. I'm not in the habit of saving girls foolish enough to put their lives in danger with the forest folk."

Rage erupted in my chest. "Thank you? Thank you? Is that what you've done? Save me?"

"Yes!" The syllable cracked through the air between us. "I will keep you here for the time being so they don't come after you again."

"You killed that boy..."

"He was feeding you fairy fruit. You would have wasted away and died, unable to leave this side of the barrier, unable to tell your friends goodbye. Is that what you want?" His handsome face had gone feral, something unearthly and powerful in his gaze.

I quailed. None of this made sense. I just wanted to go home and have Lizzie beside me. My arms started trembling.

Something he had said stood out to me suddenly. "You're going to keep me here?" my voice had grown pathetically small. I wasn't strong like Lizzie, or even like Mother, who probably would have spit in the goblin man's face to get back to her daughters.

"You're welcome," he declared, gesturing to someone behind me. I half-expected another bag to cover my head but none did. "Let's go. The girl needs to get some rest."

He stalked back in the direction we'd come with long, sure strides. Now that he didn't dominate my vision, I finally noticed the rest of my surroundings. Dark wood with marble accents formed intricate patterns in the walls and over archways. Sconces in the shapes of lifelike animals reared up, gleaming, from the walls. On the tall ceiling hung lanterns mirroring the walls' designs. A large fireplace flamed with life across from an enormous bed laid with dark blue covers trimmed in the marble's shade of pure white. Just across from where I stood were a sitting area with two chairs against a table and, inlaid into the floor by two steps, a circular pool of water.

"But—"

He stopped walking and fixed me again with those unearthly eyes. "You'll stay here tonight. Tomorrow, I'll figure out what to do with you."

Speechless, I stared after him and another similarly clad figure as they retreated from the room, locked the door from the outside, and left me alone.

❧ 6 ❧

The next morning, I woke up in silken sheets. The pillow smelled like earthy spices. I groaned and hugged its smoothness closer to my face to take in its scent.

Hit by the feeling of wrongness, I shot up in bed, feeling like a sailor who had drifted off in rough seas to find himself alone in an ocean of blue.

The shoulder of my torn and filthy nightdress drooped to my elbow, exposing the faded gold designs Lizzie had painted on me before the dance. The coolness of stone touched my skin and I shivered. Although it was summer, this room felt like it must be underground.

I swam out from beneath the covers. I'd never touched fabric so fine, and feared I must have soiled it. I had no idea what the person I'd met the night before might be capable of. He still might kill me.

Tomorrow, I'll figure out what to do with you.

I wrapped my arms around myself, slipping to the cold floor in my bare feet. My dirty shoes stood next to each other near the foot of the bed, incongruous against all this feral luxury.

Padding quickly to the door, I pulled the carved handle. The dark metal looked like a bear. The door didn't budge. I tried harder, keeping quiet in case any of the man's subordinates were outside. The lock held and the massive door was far too thick for me to kick in.

There was no way for me to tell what time it was, but I suspected it was morning. Without anything else to do, I set to exploring the space further. Maybe there was another way out. The fire had died to smoky embers, but the smell was pleasant.

The most intriguing aspect of the room was the sunken pool. Its dark blue water swirled as though stirred by an unseen hand. Apprehensive, I touched the water's surface. It was gloriously warm. I jerked my hand back in surprise. How could it have stayed hot so long if the water sat in this cold room? Fearing magic, I moved on.

Past the pool was a basin and a wardrobe I hadn't noticed last night. Inside the wardrobe were four sets of clothes. I pulled out each one to look closer. All of them seemed to have been cut for a woman to wear. Two were dresses, one long and silky blue like the sheets, and the other blood red. I normally wore wool, and I had one cotton dress for special occasions—the one I'd worn to the dance with Lizzie. Never had I seen dresses so fine. The embroidery of constellations across the deep blue gown baffled me. They seemed too small, too perfect, for human hands to make; and, even if they could, why would they? And on the maroon dress, leather crisscrossed the bodice in patterns as intricate as the ones on the walls. The result would surely be too revealing on me if I put it on. In addition to the dresses, there was a pair of slim trousers and a matching brown shirt, almost boyish. Finally, I held up a black nightgown, soft and thin as a petal, too short to be seemly.

Confused, I returned the items and did my best to wash up in the basin. I searched for a pin in the wardrobe and other corners of the large room but found none. Through a series of tucks, I managed to get my dress to stay in approximately the same shape that it'd had before my encounter with the forest creatures.

I bit my lip at the memory. I'd been a fool. The dark man had been right about that. I'd willingly put myself in danger. *What must Mother be thinking now?* I tried to shut out the thought. It was too painful, and there was nothing I could do about it until someone opened that door.

Almost as though I'd willed it, a key scraped in the lock. I stood, unsure of what to do, wishing I had my book to smash someone on the head if I had need.

To my surprise, an old woman entered. Lines filled her face, but she still had the ethereal beauty of everyone else I'd met. Keen gilded eyes met mine and I felt sure she had more life in her than I did in me at that moment. She wore a long green dress draped so cunningly I couldn't see the seams.

Joining her hands together in front of her, she said, "It's time to come to breakfast."

I didn't know what I had expected. "Breakfast?" I repeated, my voice course compared to her cultured one.

"Do you not eat breakfast?"

I couldn't tell if she was teasing, mocking, or simply didn't know. "I do eat breakfast."

So, it was not time for my death, then. My time in the grand bedroom had done nothing but bewilder me. If they didn't plan to kill me, then what? The man—or whatever he was—clearly didn't care about my sister, so why did he keep me alive, in a room with sumptuous women's clothes?

I had nothing but questions as I followed the old woman out the door.

"What's your name?" I asked, realizing I hadn't asked anyone else that question and that nobody had asked me.

"Ellis," she answered, the *s* so silvery that I thought it the prettiest name I'd never heard.

"I'm Laura," I offered. The woman barely acknowledged me.

The hallway, which I hadn't seen the night before, was made almost entirely of light marble with even more elaborate light fixtures on the walls at exact intervals. This sconce showed fighting falcons and that one the home of a family of mice. One portrayed a proud stag so lifelike I expected it to blink. The shuddering firelight made its wet eyes fairly quiver with reality.

Though the hall was enormous, still with a distinctly underground feeling, we passed no one else.

"This way."

I'd almost missed the turn Ellis was now silently treading down. I hurried to follow. A few more turns later brought us to a wooden door with the shape of a badger or wolverine adorning the center in beaten gold.

Such luxury here! I feared to touch anything, and, despite trying to pay attention the night before to the twistings of my journey down the stairs, I knew I could never find my way out alone.

Ellis pushed open the door, which swung open soundlessly. Did it even use hinges? Yes, curls of metal wrought like leaves held the door in place, but the construction was so fine they didn't squeal or protest.

At the sight inside, I gasped. A feast that dwarfed the forest creatures' offerings adorned a long wooden table. Eggs and savory pies, juices and fried meats, berries and pastries—all heaped steaming on multi-tiered dishes. My mouth watered uncontrollably at the smell.

When Ellis didn't instruct me what to do, I asked, "Where is everyone?"

She looked at me sharply. "What do you mean?"

"I mean, there's so much food..." Was Lizzie here after all? Had my dark-haired captor lied?

"Take what you like," she said dismissively, settling in a chair by a plate of stuffed dates like a woman who was already full.

Instantly, suspicion took hold. All my life, I'd heard about fairy food. The song played, strong and irresistible, in my mind:

Dear, you should not stay so late,
Twilight is not good for maidens;
Should not loiter in the glen
In the haunts of goblin men.

I sat a few chairs away from Ellis, at which point she returned her attention to me. When she didn't look away, I began to gather items on a golden plate in front of me. My stomach rumbled, betraying the truth of my hunger. Could I eat nothing here? Perhaps the savory pies wouldn't hold as much danger as the fruit. I plunked one on my plate.

"I see you prefer to stay filthy," interjected a low, refined voice that I recognized from last night.

I hadn't heard the door open. Was everyone here a ghost? I shivered at the idea that someone might have come into my room last night to put clothes in the wardrobe. Otherwise, how could they have had my size prepared?

The man, lord, whatever he was, strode in wearing an immaculate dark suit and bright gold ornaments encasing the outer rim of each ear, ending in a point at the top. His tall, muscular frame looked regal this morning, instead of fierce and murderous, as he had before. All blood had been washed away from his long fingers, though his golden eyes still had the wariness of a warrior. He turned those eyes on me.

I stiffened.

"Eat the food," he commanded as he sat on the other side of the table. "It's not poisoned or enchanted. Unless you'd rather starve. Your decision-making so far has not been exemplary."

There were so many delicacies that I had to look between towers of strawberry pastry to see him.

His attention shot to Ellis, whom I had momentarily forgotten about. "Did anyone else see her?"

"No."

"Or discover that she's in the castle?"

"No."

"Good." Almost distractedly, he began loading meat pies and pear slices with honey onto his plate. "Now we need to keep it that way."

My throat tightened. I cleared it to make way for speaking. "Excuse me, but I must find my sister—"

He set his wrists on the table and met my eyes. "Where did you get those marks?"

"Wh—what?"

"Those marks. On your arm. Where did they come from?" He asked the question so forcefully that he seemed to have been holding it back before. This was what he really wanted to know.

Self-consciously, I covered one shoulder with my hand. "My sister drew them," I said, emphasizing the words. "They're warding spells."

He scoffed, the first hint of a smile I'd seen passing his lips. "Who told you that?"

I glowered at him. Lord or not, this being with his arrogance and carelessness was trying my every nerve. I just wanted to find Lizzie and go home. I didn't care about him and my marks. Terror and worry and confusion bubbled up into anger. "My family told me that, and they have been safe for years. For generations! Until last night. So will you please let me go find my sister and make sure she's safe? I won't tell anyone I was here. Just, please, I need to leave."

"That's not possible." Totally unconcerned, he took a bite of pear. "And you didn't answer my first question. Where did you learn them?"

"My family—"

"Specifically."

I ground my teeth. I had surprised myself with my outburst and he didn't look as if he would brook a second one. I'd seen him stab and kill someone without warning yesterday. He didn't look armed today, but I knew I ought to be more careful. "There is a book of spells and charms we keep in the house. We don't use it very much."

"But that," he insisted, "that is in a language different from what you speak." He laughed mirthlessly to himself. "Obviously. So where did you acquire that one?" He gestured with a golden-tined fork toward my bare shoulder.

"I don't know."

Irritation transformed his handsome features from controlled, tight-edged calm to something more urgent, as though I were defying him.

"I don't know," I repeated. "Perhaps I could go home and ask, send a message to you somehow with the answer..."

"Do you want to be killed?" he snarled. "You cannot go back. I don't know why you decided to paint yourself and then go into the forest in the first place, if you want to go home so badly now."

"Endymion," the old woman admonished. "She clearly doesn't understand. It does no good to berate her."

"You know we can't take her back," he challenged, one dark eyebrow rising.

"I do."

"But," I said, unable to help myself, "why not?"

Endymion—my captor now had a name—ignored me, instead focusing on Ellis. His eyes blazed. "I'll see to it that those marks are gone and then we can decide what to do with her."

He'd said the same last night and the tingling on my skin echoed back the same fear: *He'll kill me.* I had no idea why the marks were so important or why they refused to listen to me. They acted as if I were a burden to them, yet they wouldn't let me go. Surely, that could only mean one outcome.

Sucking in a deep, frustrated breath, Endymion turned back to me, lip curling. The ornaments on his ears gleamed in the light of a low chandelier I hadn't noticed until then. "Did you eat any fairy fruit last night?"

My head whirled with so many odd changes in topic. "I don't think so." Although I'd washed my face in the basin that morning, the enticing smell lingered on me. Oddly, he seemed to notice, even from the other side of the table.

Surprise washed his features at my answer, his forceful gaze dropping to my mouth for a moment.

"Well, that is something," said Ellis. She shared a look with Endymion that I couldn't begin to read.

The memory of the fruit in the forest only stoked my hunger. I squeezed my middle to keep it from growling. "You said last night that I would be unable to leave this side of the barrier if I had eaten it. But I didn't," I reasoned.

"No," he said brusquely. "I know what you're thinking. You cannot go home. Is your room not good enough for you?"

I swallowed against welling emotion. Lizzie, Mother, Grandmother, even Great-grandmother pressed on my mind so force-fully I thought I might collapse.

Endymion rose, leaving most of his food untouched. "Send her back to her room with a tray of food. I have too many things to do without this." He muttered the last part to himself, running a hand through his dark hair. Then, louder, "I'll return tonight for answers to my questions."

Dazed, I felt the room spin. My whole world was questions, and I didn't know where to begin. I just knew I needed to get out of here and back home where I belonged. Hopefully Lizzie was safe and I was the only one captured by a cruel lord. The opulent feast blurred and I tottered to one side.

I heard a soft curse before strong hands stopped me from falling to the floor.

❧ 7 ❧

It was my twentieth birthday today. Perhaps Mother had a little spice cake ready for me in case I returned. I certainly hadn't expected to spend today locked in a lavish room at the behest of a powerful otherworldly being.

An hour ago, when I'd come to, my eyes cracked open to see Endymion standing over me, regal face full of consternation. He scowled at Ellis, utterly placid beside him near the big blue bed where I lay. "Did you hear the name correctly? It was Laura, not Laurel or some such thing? She does not respond when I use—"

"She's awake." Ellis met my eyes. "Eat, Laura." She gestured a graceful hand toward a platter of food next to me on the bed. "We are glad to see you well."

The two of them shared another familiar glance and, for the first time, I realized how they appeared similar enough to be related.

Endymion heaved a breath and exited without another word.

I slowly sat up, my head throbbing dully.

Ellis turned to leave also, but the questions churning through my mind after the almost-breakfast made me call out.

Forehead raised, she regarded me again.

"Where is this place?" I asked, voice oddly husky.

"You are in Tylaith Castle."

I had never heard of it before. "And you...?" I didn't know how to ask what they were. By now, I was convinced they weren't forest creatures. Endymion was as different from the fawn-boy as I was from a cat.

"We are Fae," she answered, a hint of amusement on her face. "And yes, Endymion is the King."

The thought was so strange. Ellis didn't offer her relationship to him, but I guessed she might be his mother. According to legend, Fae didn't age, or if they did, it was so slowly that generations of humans couldn't detect it. They had mysterious magic as well, not clearly delineated in our conflicting tales. Their beauty was cause for seduction and terror, though whether they were good or evil shifted depending on the story.

Since Ellis seemed to be in an answering mood, I persisted. "What does he want with the markings?" He could be capable of lopping off my arm to get to them, but he hadn't harmed me so far.

"That is for him to tell you."

I bit the inside of my lip.

"Eat," she said again, and left me alone.

Despite the warnings and songs, I finally ate. The food was unlike anything I'd eaten before, spiced with flavors I'd never experienced and bursting with decadent juices. I stopped just shy of sickness.

My headache subsided. Before I could rise from the silken covers of the bed to check the lock, the door opened and three young women emerged, identically dressed in gauzy white. One carried a plush towel with something glossy thrown over it, another a set of brushes, and the last a tray with several miniature bottles. Each woman could have stolen my breath on her own, but the effect of seeing three such gorgeous creatures made me shier than usual. I felt unbearably plain next to their glowing skin and strong bodies. They moved with the grace of dancers.

"Is Miss ready for her bath?" asked the one with the towel.

"Pardon?" I stuttered.

"We are here to assist you."

Finally, what they were saying sank in. Even more self-conscious, I drew the dark blue coverlet up to my chest. "I don't need any help."

"The King has sent us." The Fae girl's words quashed any opposition I could offer.

Awkwardly, I let them lead me to the circular pool in the center of the room. With practiced hands, they removed my torn dress and folded it on the floor. Their expressions remained neutral, not gawking or mocking, although I knew myself far less magnificent than they were. I stepped into the warm water. Its effect was immediate. Comfort soaked into my bones and I held back a groan of pleasure, sinking up to my neck in the swirling water.

The young women scrubbed me with the brushes and took out my gnarled braid before combing spiced oil through my hair. One girl focused almost entirely on my shoulder. She rubbed different soaps and tinctures on it and scoured it until it felt raw. The faded golden symbols stubbornly remained, even when my red skin felt as though it had been flayed.

"Please," I finally said, "stop."

The girl at my shoulder stared back at me. "The King says these must be gone."

Now that the bath had lost some of its comforting qualities, I had my mind about me again. "Why does he want them gone? What do they say?"

The trio looked at one another before answering. "It is the prophecy, Miss."

"Prophecy?"

"About the war. It is the prophecy the whole kingdom knows."

Looks of realization crossed their glowing faces when I still didn't understand. They too had golden eyes.

"We should not have said anything," said the one at my shoulder, redoubling her effort to scrub the symbols away. "You will forgive us."

"Ouch!" I said, flinching away.

"Perhaps we could cover it for now," one suggested uncertainly.

I was already leaving the bath, struggling to get away from the ruthless brush scraping my shoulder. A towel was draped around me and their ministrations became soothing again. Scented lotions stung the area where the golden brush had painted, but felt luscious everywhere else. Despite the discomfort and the purpose behind this cleaning, between that and the morning feast, I felt more indulgent than I ever had before.

"Did you have any of the feast?" I asked, suddenly aware of the sheer wastefulness of it all.

Shining eyes regarded me strangely. "Feast?" they asked.

"In the dining room. There was so much food. I hope you were able to eat some of it."

They didn't reply, but I had the sense that they hadn't enjoyed any of it. Perhaps Fae didn't often eat. Perhaps these magnificent young women were lowly servants not allowed to eat such food.

One moved away on her long legs toward the fireplace where the flames had gone out.

The other two began to dry my long blonde hair and put salve on my calloused hands. They pared and buffed my broken fingernails. I couldn't help wondering what all this fuss was for. Though the room smelled delicious and my skin glowed almost as radiantly as the Fae attendants' did, unease pierced me now. Was I a pretty sacrifice to a savage god?

They drew out the maroon gown with leather fittings.

"What do you mean, it won't come off?" demanded a now familiar voice.

I grasped my towel from where I'd let it fall and covered myself. How dare Endymion burst in while I was bathing?

He stalked up to me. Again, I understood the myths of Fae seduction. Even angry, his handsome face, tending toward wickedness, and his strong physique called for me to admire. Though I felt too small in the room, he looked like the correct size for it. Behind him strode the Fae girl who had stoked the fire. The others at my sides parted like oil from water. I stood alone before the King, covered in nothing but a towel.

His carved lip curled as he glared at my shoulder, wetness from my hair dripping over it. He gripped the place where my markings were, roughly at first, then searchingly, scraping his thumb across my already raw skin.

"What did you do?" he accused, releasing me.

"I did nothing." I fought to keep from trembling under his stare. I had no idea why the symbols weren't washing off. They always had before.

He worked his jaw, considering.

"What do they say?" I said, voice almost breaking, but I kept eye contact with him. "What war are the symbols talking about?"

"What war..." His eyes rolled as he scoffed the words. "You humans don't even know how close you've come to devastation and you ask what war."

"Then tell me."

He returned my look, his eyes hard chips of amber. "Im

Scathail." The rumbling words emerged like darkness made audible.

Blood heating, I held the towel tighter around myself.

"The Sleeper. The Enemy." He stepped even closer, towering above me. I could see the fine threading of his black suit. "The one you have no hope to fight, no matter what little plan you thought you had running into the woods."

"Wait, what?"

"Don't pretend ignorance, Laura. I don't intend to let you go spreading rumors." Snapping his focus back to the attendants, he said, "Cover it. See that no one else knows."

My heart hammered as he touched me again, scraping my shoulder lightly with his fingernail. My nerves quivered as if a blade had idly scraped my skin instead. With a sigh, he backed away.

My previous sense of luxury had vanished like a soap bubble. Now I stood shivering with cool water running down my naked back and my shoulder protesting against the pain of so much scrubbing and prodding.

He left without more explanation.

The sensation of Endymion's fingernail lingered far longer than it should have.

❧   8   ❧

I needed answers.

Left alone again for hours, I mulled over everything Endymion and the attendants had said. The symbols on my shoulder were a prophecy relating to a war against someone called Im Scathail. The King didn't believe that I was ignorant of the symbols' origins and what they said. Everyone among the Fae knew the prophecy, allegedly. If I could get someone to tell me...

Suppertime had to be approaching by now and I was no closer to unraveling the riddle of what was happening to me. Nor did I have any sign of Lizzie. I half-expected her to open the grand door and smirk at me as though this had all been a game. We would run back to the cottage together.

Warm tears bit my eyes. I wiped them away and rubbed the side of my hands on the blood-red dress I'd been given to wear. It did plunge in front and on the sides, the bodice crossed with a complicated network of leather straps holding it in place. The skirt floated over the floor as I paced.

When the door swung inward, I halted. A Fae man, dressed in the close dark leather outfit Endymion had worn in the forest, entered. He might have been with the King that night. His rugged, dark face looked a little familiar.

"Laura?"

"Yes?" For someone so adamant about keeping me a secret, Endymion certainly informed many people I was here.

"I'm Calyse. The King has commanded me to allow you free reign of the lower apartment. His kindness, he hopes, will not go unrewarded."

I hoped he meant *with information.*

Calyse's brows were heavier than Endymion's, and his aspect less threatening, despite wearing what could have been armor. In fact, his eyes—orange as a cat's—had a joke in them.

"Thank you," I managed. Sleeves covered the golden marks on my arm, but Calyse's eyes still lingered on my shoulder.

"You are not to go upstairs."

"All right."

"May you sleep short and live long," he said abruptly in the tone of a blessing, though I didn't see how sleeping less could be a favorable thing to wish on someone. With a nod of his head that allowed me to see a starburst pattern radiating from his forehead through the thick strands of his black hair, he left, leaving the door wide open.

This had to be a trap. I hadn't begged for greater access. Once Calyse disappeared down a bend in the hall, I saw no one else. Remembering how labyrinthine the corridors had been when I followed Ellis to the dining room, I resolved, as always, to be careful.

But I also resolved to escape.

After waiting several long minutes listening for anyone who might be lurking in the passage, I bolted out. I gathered my skirt in my hand to keep it from tripping me in my haste. The white marble hallway echoed as empty as a tomb. My shoes made slapping noises against the stone floor, even though I attempted to quiet them. More than once, Fae had appeared without any preamble of sound. My mortal clumsiness made that level of stealth impossible for me. Regardless, here was a chance to run, so I took it, darting into each branching hallway methodically, trying not to lose my way. None of the doors I encountered would open, no matter how hard I pulled the carved metal handles.

Not that one. Not that one.

Could Lizzie be somewhere in this maze of halls, locked in as I had been?

I tugged a handle sculpted like tree branches with a watchful owl atop them. When the door gave, my pulse jogged in my throat. I peeked around the door to make sure no one was inside. I saw no Fae, forest creatures, or humans. What I did see were books, hundreds of them lined on dark wooden shelves. Their leather and fabric spines glowed with silver and precious stones and, of course, gold. I slipped inside, shutting the door softly behind me.

The room was smaller than the enormous space allotted to me, rounded on one side and angular on the other. Everywhere I looked were warm browns and rich greens giving off the peppery smell of parchment.

A few times, I'd visited Lizzie at the bookbinder's. The smell there was nothing to the caramel and smoke scent here.

A table in the center of the room held two volumes spread open to unreadable pages. Although I recognized some titles along the floor to ceiling bookshelves, the symbols on the table matched those on my arm instead. I ran a finger lightly against the creamy parchment, worn brittle at the edges. These books might hold some of the answers I wanted.

So far, I'd found no way out. I could at least arm myself with a better understanding of what was going on.

A spike of longing struck me for the book Lizzie had created especially for my birthday. Where was it now? Would I ever hold the tales of Orlando and Genevieve in my hands again?

Shaking off the thought, I focused on the hardbound books on the shelves. Some of them I could read. Sconces mounted on the shelves' supporting beams cast flickering light along the spines. I pulled down *Campaigns of Nox*, *The Great War*, and *The Relative Utility of Earth Spells*. Something in these volumes had to tell me more about the Fae war against Im Scathail, and perhaps one would even include the prophecy.

I settled into an oversized chair plush and green as moss, and began to read.

I did not find the prophecy. Details of the war, though, splashed bloody through the pages. Whole cities razed, families mutilated, generations sent into enchanted sleep... I'd never heard such horrors, even in stories. Darkness crept like sickness, impervious to campaigns of war.

I was shaking by the time I set down the first book. How was it possible that humans didn't know about this menace? Had the stories simply been lost to time? As far as I could tell, the conflict had persisted through time out of mind, before humans even settled in Selene and the farther cities.

What did my family's warding charm have to do with any of this? Were the forest creatures in league with Im Scathail? It didn't seem possible. When I'd met them, they were wild and debauched, but didn't seem particularly evil. Perhaps I was naïve. I liked to think that everyone would choose the side of right if given the chance, even those who sometimes enjoyed breaking the rules.

Gingerly replacing the books on the shelves, I exited silently and tried the last few doors but, as I suspected, they too were all locked, even the dining room. I couldn't shake the feeling that, although Calyse had given me permission to leave the room, it must be illicit to roam the halls. Endymion hadn't hesitated to skewer the fawn-boy. He could very well do the same to me if I displeased him more than I had already.

No one else came to me that day. I wandered out periodically when I thought it was safe. Around meal times—by my internal measure, anyway—I made sure to be in my room. A platter of game bird adorned with juicy plums was set inside the door at supper. I didn't see by whom. Though I tried every door and started to get a good sense of the layout of this glorious marble tomb, I never discovered stairs leading up or any doors leading out. My cage had only widened.

On each excursion, I stopped at the little library. Not only did it possibly hold my connection to this terrible, shadowy Fae war, but it also felt more like home than anything had since Lizzie had fallen asleep with me after the dance.

❧   9   ☙

Days passed. Someone entered every morning to ask me the same questions. Where had I learned those symbols? Why did I go into the woods that night? Why won't the symbols come off? Every day, I answered the same way. With the truth. This didn't please any of my questioners, who rotated among Ellis and Calyse and Endymion himself.

Once they were gone, I knew I had hours to conduct my own investigation before the beautiful attendants came again to wash me and put new potions or scrubs on my shoulder to clean off the letters left by the golden brush.

The books in the library didn't yield the allegedly famous prophecy, or, at least, it didn't clarify which prophecy it was. There were many, mostly forecasting destruction in enough varieties to make me want to hide under the silken blue covers and never emerge. If even a fraction of those prophecies were true, then not only was battle coming to the Fae and mortal lands, but large-scale desolation.

A couple of interesting facts stood out among the books I could read, that weren't in the strange characters permanently etched on my arm. Calyse's parting words made better sense after I learned that, one hundred and twenty years ago, the Fae had slept for thirty years in an enchanted sleep that threatened to annihilate them. Their bodies and memories began to waste away because of the effect of Im Scathail's curse.

May you sleep short and live long.

The second piece of information I learned was the identity of the prophetess herself. All prophecies concerning the war seemed to come from the same mouth. She was known only as the Oakmaiden. I couldn't be sure if she still lived, but, judging from the nearly immortal Fae, I wouldn't have been surprised. Perhaps if I couldn't find the answer in books, I could someday seek out the Oakmaiden in person.

Mulling on these things as I lay in bed, the remaining mysteries haunted me. I wanted answers. I wanted to escape. I needed to find Lizzie. Helplessness threatened to crush me. I was no fighter who could force my way out. I wasn't cunning enough to bypass a series of thick locked doors. I was a gardener from Selene who had never wanted to go into the woods in the first place.

Even the sumptuous softness of the blankets couldn't lull me to sleep. I sat up. Better to make use of this otherwise wasted time. The wood and marble floor cooled my bare feet as I stepped to the unlocked door. As always, the sconces were lit, though I never heard anyone refill the oil, if indeed that was how they burned. I crossed my arms against the seeping chill. The black nightdress I wore was poor insulation.

There had been a book with a chapter about insignias that might be helpful. I knew it was a slim hope, but I held onto each slim hope as it arrived.

I pulled the owl handle and crept inside. My core froze.

There, in the green armchair, wearing an open shirt and

tousled hair, wreathed in black shadows, sat Endymion. He was reading my book.

He blinked at me in surprise. In my panic, I vaguely registered the glass of amber liquid on the end table beside him. The shadows around him curled like smoke, winding around the open pages in his hand. I'd never seen those shadows before. I would have remembered them.

"How did you get out of your room?"

I didn't know how to reply. My instinct that he wouldn't encourage my exploration was confirmed. I felt like I'd been caught stealing.

His eyes narrowed and cut to the side. "Calyse," he hissed. "Of course. He knew better than to let you out." Then he released a breath and settled more deeply into the chair, turning his gaze once again to me. The chair looked like a throne with him in it, despite his disheveled appearance.

He snapped the book closed, shadows puffing from its pages like smoke from a fallen log. I cried out in protest before I could stop myself.

"What's done cannot be undone," he said in a clipped voice. "Now that you're here, perhaps you can tell me the significance of this book. Who are these people?" He held up the volume Lizzie had bound for me.

Unwanted emotion rose up at the sight of it. "It's nothing. It's just stories..."

"Orlando and Genevieve are not real?"

I gave a sad laugh at the absurdity of all this. "No. They're not real."

"But the gold on the cover is the same as the pigment used on your skin," he persisted.

"That doesn't make the characters real."

Endymion rubbed his temple in a gesture wearier than any I'd seen from him. The untidy hair hanging over his face fairly flamed with shadows. I lost his edges when I tried to see them straight on. "Why do you invent tragedy where there is none?"

At this, I stood speechless. No one but Lizzie ever talked to me about my secret passions—I cringed to think which passages this King must have read. Finally, I found my voice. "I suppose I do it to remind myself that life has worth, despite tragedy. Their love..." I faltered. How much of this did he want to hear? "It didn't stop mattering because their lives were cut short. Love was sweeter because of it."

Endymion's golden eyes had gone as blurry as his edges, but not from tears. I suspected it was from drink or exhaustion. Regardless, his attention hadn't wavered from me. His focus was so intense that my chest and face flushed warm the longer he stared. Heart thundering, I realized I wore only my nightgown.

"Love doesn't exist," he declared, with the air of someone throwing away all caution. I was certain now of his having too many drinks. "That's what they want, what they think will solve all this. That damn prophecy." He pointed at my shoulder with his long fingers.

I held my breath.

"As if marrying a mortal woman could solve anything."

My lips parted in surprise. The war. The prophecy. It said that the war could end if he married a human?

"That's what you want, isn't it?"

Reeling, I met his glare. "No! I didn't know."

"I don't want a wife." He bit out each word as though he'd already repeated it endlessly to someone who wouldn't listen.

I knew the feeling. "That's not why I'm here!"

"Then why are you here, if not to share my bed and magically end the war?"

My gut somersaulted. No one had said such things to me. "To find my sister Lizzie."

"Ah, the one who ate the fairy fruit." He waved his hand dismissively, leaning back into the chair cushion.

I scowled. "We don't know that." But in my heart I feared it must be true. Poor Lizzie... An idea struck me, obvious as the sun. How could I have not thought of it before? "She might know more about the symbols and the golden brush. She's a year older than I am. Perhaps Mother told her the secret of how our family discovered those things." The words poured out, fast and desperate.

Endymion's eyebrow twitched. When he clasped his hands together in his lap, darkness steamed around them. "Lizzie"—his voice slurred a little—"is gone."

"How do you know?" I wrung my hands to keep them from shaking too visibly.

"She could not have survived."

"I did," I challenged.

"You are the only one in lifetimes I have managed to come across in time."

"Maybe you should look harder." My words were reckless now. Endymion brought out a side of me I hardly recognized. "Maidens in Selene go missing every year."

"Is love sweeter because of the brevity of their lives?"

I recoiled from his cruel repetition. Breaths came hard and fast. My throat worked but no retort emerged.

Insolently, he held out the book. As if in a dream, I moved to take it from him. The shadows curling around his body caressed my hand as I took back the only memento left of my sister.

A week after my encounter with Endymion in the library, no one had come to ask me any more questions. Ellis visited once. The three attendants cleaned me several more times to no avail. More dresses appeared in my wardrobe, though when or who put them there, I never knew. There was a silvery gray gown with leather accents and a diaphanous pink gown I feared would be totally transparent.

I still snuck out of my room, though even more carefully than before. The doors, all but one, save mine, were always locked. I only went to the library during what seemed to be daylight hours, fearing Endymion would be seated there as before, petulant and dissolute. My dislike for him grew hourly. Not only did he kidnap me and show no regard for my missing sister, but he also made a horrific war drag on because he didn't believe in love. I'd never heard something so absurd. From the hints he dropped on the night in the library, all he had to do was marry a mortal girl and the war would end. But he refused. I wasn't planning to offer up myself, but surely there was a good opportunity and a willing participant who could have stopped all the horror I read about.

Despair threatened to crush me. I slept longer hours, even mindful of Calyse's blessing of a short sleep. With little else to do this evening, I stripped naked and stepped into the churning pool in the center of my room. Warm water enveloped my skin. At least my body could be comforted, if not my mind.

Tales of Orlando and Genevieve sat at the edge of the pool, away from any water droplets. Reading it had sounded too painful after Endymion's pronouncement that Lizzie was dead, but today I thought I'd try. I rested my elbows on the edge of the pool and began.

Once upon a time, there lived a shepherd named Orlando. The shepherd worked in the fields within sight of the castle called Roset. Within Roset dwelled a maiden named Genevieve. Every day, she looked out the window of her high tower, longing to know more of the world. From birth, her parents, caretakers, and servants had fed her with the finest foods and presented her with beautiful animals and toys to play with. Musicians played her songs and acrobats danced at her birthday. But she was lonely and knew nothing of the world outside. From her window, she could watch Orlando, the handsome shepherd, sing rustic songs to the sheep. Once, he fought off a wolf, valiantly protecting the flock with his bravery. Over time, Genevieve fell in love with him...

I squinted and peered more closely at the margins, where black scrawl as thin as spider's legs ran slanting up the parchment. These weren't mistakes made at the bookbinder, but notes.

Where is Roset? one of the first notes asked.

Does fairy fruit prevent her from leaving? Then, next to the last sentence on that page: *Poor cure for loneliness.*

Endymion had written notes all throughout my book. Heat that had nothing to do with my bath roared through my veins. This was *my* book. I had written it; my sister had bound it. I didn't like the idea of the Fae King reading it, much less writing in it. There were self-indulgent passages in later stories about the couple that revealed too many of my darker longings, inelegantly disguised within the characters.

I flipped through the rest of the uneven pages. Endymion had annotated it all.

When Genevieve, after saying a heartfelt farewell to her lover, succumbed to the fatal bite of the myur, a snake creature set on her by the wicked goblin men, Endymion had savagely crossed out the final paragraphs.

I closed the book. I couldn't look anymore. He defiled my story, the last memory of my sister, if what he said was true.

"You appear busy."

I cried out and hugged the side of the pool, trying to cover myself.

Calyse stood above me in the doorway, a smirk on his face. His thick strands of hair had been pulled back in a knotted bun in the back of his head. Today, instead of wearing the tight leather armor I'd seen a few times, he sported a regal-looking cream suit with blue accents that perfectly highlighted his rich brown skin.

Did the entire Fae culture not care about privacy?

"I *am* busy," I said, choked up with anger from my recent findings.

"Come to supper with me," he declared, holding out a hand. "I know Endymion is a pest, but that doesn't mean you can't emerge for some company once in a while." His fiery eyes looked sincere, as far as the Fae went.

I frowned skeptically.

"I'm curious to get to know you. We don't get any human girls staying with us. End is currently too... preoccupied to treat you as a guest." *End.* Did Fae have nicknames as humans did? Calyse said the King's name with such familiarity that she had to guess they were friends, at least, more than King and soldier. "I've bothered him about it, but he's stubborn."

The look of shock on Endymion's face that day in the library made more sense. He hadn't ordered that I be free to explore the lower floor. Calyse had acted on his own.

"Come on," he pressed, eyes sparkling in a mischievous way that contrasted sharply with his rugged warrior appearance. "Get some clothes on and meet me in the dining room. I know you know where it is."

Despite his disarming manner, I felt unnerved by the invitation. I'd been treated as a prisoner, a shameful secret, someone to eventually be eliminated unless I could figure out a way to prove useful.

Well, if Calyse was willing to talk to me...

"And End is gone for a week," he clarified.

My uncertainty subsided. I would love some company for supper if I didn't have to face the King I hated.

❧

I chose the silver dress and found the dining room without a problem. Calyse was already there, smiling and talking to Ellis in the cheery light from the chandelier. The dark cloud of Endymion's glower was gone. This place did not look half as menacing without him.

"There you are," Calyse greeted, pulling out a chair. On the table were savory squashes topped with nuts, slices of ham, braided breads glistening with butter, and a bowls of peas and asparagus. I couldn't name the other dishes.

"Thank you," I said, settling into the seat. My braid was still wet from the bath. Compared to these stunning people, I felt flimsy.

"She speaks!" Calyse laughed, taking his place opposite me. Ellis sat at the head where she had sat before when I'd visited this room. I couldn't help noticing that their outlines were as clear as mine, not obscured by shadows as I'd seen on Endymion the other night.

"I'm sorry we have to keep you locked away. It was quite a night when we found you," he exclaimed, filling his plate.

Ellis caught my eye and gestured that I was allowed to do the same.

I reached immediately for the bread and ham. I'd long since given up the idea that the Fae were feeding me cursed fairy fruit. Even if they had been, what choice did I have?

"That prophecy on your arm—I know you must be worn out hearing about it—took us all by surprise. The forest folk circulate it among themselves, of course, but I hadn't seen a record of it in, oh..." He tipped his generous mouth. "It must be a century."

Calyse didn't look older than mid-thirties. I was struck anew with a sense of being alien among them.

"It says something about how marriage could help end the war with Im Scathail. Am I right?" I asked quietly. Ellis was never in a sharing mood, but Calyse seemed happy to talk.

"Ooh!" Calyse crooned. "So you do know what it says. Yes, the forest folk have never let it go. Ever since the Oakmaiden said it the first time, those creatures have latched onto it like bark on tree."

"If they already know about it, why is the King worried about them seeing the words on me?"

Calyse bit into a hunk of ham. "This sort of thing could send his subjects into a frenzy. We can't have that happen."

"A frenzy? Why?" I marveled at how much easier it was to talk to Calyse than Endymion, always so cold to me.

"They'll see it as a sign. The prophecy written on a mortal woman? Literally on the skin of a beautiful human girl?" He waggled his thick brows, inviting me to fill in the rest. "Surely, you can see how that might lead the kingdom to conclusions."

I'd never been called beautiful before. Calyse said it not as the boys of the village had said it about Lizzie, but more as a statement of fact. The sky was blue and I was beautiful. Despite the dire situation Calyse described, I warmed with pleasure at the compliment.

"The forest folk don't need more evidence to reinforce their chaos. I'm not blaming you." Calyse held out a large, conciliatory hand. "You seem as ignorant as you say."

I was glad he believed me, but he didn't need to call me ignorant. I reached for what knowledge I had to prove otherwise. "Does the King think I staged all this on purpose in order to end the war?"

If he was surprised by my depth of understanding, then it didn't show. "It's a theory, yes."

I cleared my throat. "I haven't heard the prophecy in its entirety. Does it just say that the King must marry a mortal to end the war?"

"It says that *if* he marries a mortal woman, the war will end."

I felt like the Fae was just repeating my words, but he seemed to insist on some nuance lost on me.

"Then why hasn't he?" I asked, thinking of all the horrific descriptions I'd read of famines and massacres and darkness.

Ellis cut in, her voice bitter. "The forest folk hang their every hope on that foolish prophecy. Those debauched creatures..."

"So we were, of course, glad to have been able to spare you the same fate. Though, what your fate will be now, I wish I could say."

"Same fate?" I repeated, halting.

"As the others from your village." When I still didn't understand, he went on. "The forest folk offer mortals to Endymion every year hoping he'll choose one of them. Once they're done with them, of course."

My head spun. "What?" I breathed.

All the maidens disappearing into the woods at twilight, lured by the promise of fruit, of abandon. It had all been... for Endymion? He could have stopped all of the grief my village had endured these years long if he had just chosen a bride?

"They don't know how to treat them," said Ellis, as though nothing world-shattering had just been explained to me. "Savages."

"What... what would have happened if I had eaten the fruit they offered? Would I have been sent here anyway as some kind of prize?"

Calyse's vivid eyes turned compassionate. "You don't have to worry about that now. Obviously, we don't want word to spread of your markings. That's why we have to hold you here." He looked meaningfully at Ellis. "I told you he wouldn't have said anything."

"We were holding the girl for questioning," she replied archly.

"If they know you're here, they'll demand that he marry, think that peace is near," Calyse said, his jaw tightening, world weary despite the jovial aspect I'd seen from him each time we'd interacted.

My mind still spun. I couldn't move past what they'd said earlier. I touched my shoulder lightly, covered by a mantle over my silver dress. "Doesn't that mean that the forest creatures will stop taking maidens from Selene?"

Calyse raised an eyebrow. "They'll demand he marry *you*."

I had no idea why they weren't already forcing me into doing that, given everything they'd said. My gut jumped at the thought, but if something so simple could end a centuries-long war...

I stayed silent, munching a piece of bread.

"Such serious talk with our guest!" Calyse suddenly exclaimed, pouring ruby liquid into a glass and handing it across the table to me. "I apologize. We're all frustrated with recent events. You have to excuse us. We didn't come down just to talk about our problems."

Ellis' mouth went thin as she cast a look at Calyse, who leaned his head as if to persuade her to his way of thinking. She rolled her eyes.

Calyse clasped his hands together in conspiratorial victory. "You are not, no matter how inhospitable End has been, a prisoner with us, but our guest. We're not used to having humans in the castle. I, for one, find your kind fascinating! You live such full lives before you're snuffed out."

I didn't know whether to be flattered or dismayed. This Fae wouldn't snuff me out, would he? I had the feeling he was on my side. He presented himself as someone friendly, and I couldn't be choosy about my allies.

"I'd love to show you the rest of the castle. This dingy basement isn't all the Fae have to offer!" He spread his arms, leaning back, his barrel chest puffing with pride.

I huffed a tiny laugh at his theatrics. "I would love to see the rest." If this was a "dingy basement" then I had no idea what wonders the rest must hold. I longed for Lizzie. She would have enjoyed this so much, despite the danger.

"I'll take you up tonight. But you'll have to cover your face and your markings, of course."

"That's fine," I agreed, eager to see above.

I ate the food shamefully quickly, I was so eager to go on the tour Calyse promised. Neither Ellis nor Calyse offered any more revelations during dinner. I didn't think I could have handled another.

Young women were stolen as gifts for this Fae King, who merely rejected them and let the cycle persist? It was beyond belief, beyond any basic humanity. Perhaps all the Fae were, no matter how seemingly gracious.

Though I was grateful to Calyse for showing me kindness, my disdain for Endymion grew.

With dinner over and a mask in place, I followed Calyse to a door adjacent to the dining room—I took care to note which one and the pocket from which he took his key—and followed him upstairs. Ellis left us after the meal. Perhaps she didn't want to be seen with me. Calyse, even though he had insisted on my wearing the mask, didn't seem too perturbed about that, or about possibly angering Endymion if word got out. At this point, I wasn't bothered by angering him either. Yes, the King was dangerous, but some beings deserved defiance. Bolstered by that thought, I ascended the steps.

Ahead of me on the steps, the big back of Calyse twisted and he paused. His ruggedly handsome profile showed hesitation. "End won't be happy," he said, and chuckled, "but when is he ever?" With that, he ascended the rest of the stairs to the upper part of the castle.

Veiled by my mask, I took in the scene that unfolded ahead of me. No door separated the staircase from the upper levels. My gaze went up and up and up. The ceiling was as high as the sky on a cloudy day, mostly glass or something transparent that allowed it to look like the night through tree branches. Enormous silvery stone trunks stood evenly along a colonnade so grand I feared to step into it. I couldn't tell if the trees were real or only momentous statues. Precious blue stones inlaid the smooth bark of the trees in sweeping patterns. Everywhere there was movement, Fae and forest creature and things for which I had no name. Under our feet were moss and rich marble arrayed in a pattern that suggested a walkway.

A flash of red streaked the upper part of the colonnade. A bird. Emotion clogged my throat at the beauty of it.

Calyse moved through this grand space with the comfort of a native. I hurried after him. The Fae we passed stunned me with their graceful lines, their flashing eyes, their sensuous mouths and muscled bodies. Even their hair gleamed. Yet, among them, Endymion still would have drawn the eye, especially with the gold ornaments on his ears.

A few of the Fae looked at me, the stranger among them. Their attention burned like cold metal, but none moved to unmask or question me.

Only when I was halfway down the cavernous colonnade did I realize how many of the partygoers—for, surely, this must be a party—were scarred and disfigured. Black rents like lightning scars forked down their bodies. Patches covered their eyes. Hands were blackened to cinders, surreptitiously covered by soft leather gloves.

My breathing grew shallow as I followed Calyse's cream-colored suit, keeping my eyes down. I didn't want to draw any more attention than necessary.

The sky-high ceiling began to dip and funnel into a more reasonably sized room where the roof rose only the height of three Fae if they stood end to end. My eyes could more easily reconcile my surroundings into a building. The trunks of smaller sculpted trees lined this space, branching out above our heads into a semi-level overflowing with greenery. Forest creatures, moving with the deliberation of gardeners, stirred just out of sight on the platforms.

I wanted to cry out with joy, to ask about the floating gardens, but Calyse strode too quickly. Two of my strides matched one of his.

Finally, he led me to more stairs, this time a sweeping staircase of green stone. Stately Fae, with a debauched gleam to their eye or muss to their hair, descended. The steps curved up and up, around banisters carved as beasts at every turning. At last, just as my thighs began to protest painfully against the endless climb, we halted. We had reached the top of a thin tower encased within the unimaginably huge castle. Windows paneled the circular room. Vertigo gripped me as I looked down and saw levels of gardens and dancing and combat training, kitchens and bedrooms, gazebos and indoor pools. Each being looked as neat and jeweled as a figurine. Stumbling back from the sight, I met Calyse's eyes, speechless.

"It's not bad," he exclaimed, his orange eyes shining bright as a cat's.

I understood now why they dismissed my magnificent room as part of a lowly basement.

"This is the best view in the whole castle," he went on. "It's easier to show you everything here than to rush you from place to place." His expression suggested he knew that the climb up the stairs had worn me out. "End will stand here sometimes," he mused, fearlessly peering down, "to be reminded of what we all fight for. It's easy to lose sight when you've been fighting as long as we have." He gave a dark chuckle.

"I don't understand," I admitted slowly. "The Oakmaiden gave him a way to win."

"Endymion is fighting in other ways."

I huffed out my frustration.

Calyse set a hand against my back to encourage me to look down again. "Look. I know he can seem an intransigent bastard, probably because he is, but he's fighting harder than any of us." He spoke softly, as though of a brother.

I wasn't convinced he deserved any kind feelings. The height still made me dizzy and I leaned back, but managed to keep my eyes on the view in front of me. "Those gardens," I said, pointing. "What do they grow?"

"Everything," he said vaguely. "I'm no gardener. Would you like to see?" He beamed at me, bright white teeth contrasting with his skin. "As long as you keep your markings and face covered on the upper levels, I don't see why you can't see the castle or gardens anytime you like. And if Endymion gets upset about any of it, just say I put you up to it."

◈

MAKING CHARMS GAVE ME A SMALL SENSE OF POWER AGAIN. Calyse visited my room once a day to see how I fared and to give me directions to the floating garden landings. I could take anything I wanted, he told me, as long as it wasn't in large quantities. The forest creatures, he warned, could be wily, so he advised me to accept no gifts from them and never to follow them away from the gardens. So my daily routine changed to include the gardens above as well as the rooms below. With Endymion gone for some unspecified amount of time, I had the library to myself even at night.

I'd procured a mortar and pestle from the kitchens and sat before my fireplace, grinding herbs. Warding spells would do little to protect me here, but perhaps something could help rid me of the markings and allow me to go home.

Today, I was making a healing potion. Heather and lemon balm, ginger and chamomile, crushed and then swished together, would create the necessary mixture. The sensation of tiny leaves against my calloused fingers as I stripped the stems felt like home. I clicked my tongue. Was there an ingredient I was forgetting? I felt as if I needed one more thing. I pursed my mouth and glanced at the door. The library would surely have a record of this or similar healing potions. The disfigurements I'd seen on so many of the Fae necessitated a great knowledge of healing among their kind. I set down the pestle and left to find the recipe.

Out of habit, I checked the locked doors along the way, tugging on each of the metallic creature handles. The library lay on the opposite end of the hall from my room, so there were quite a few doors between them. Always, they were locked.

But then, the cold carving of a stoat gave under my palm. My heart jogged. Unsure, I kept pulling. The door was unlocked. The room inside looked pitch black and smelled stale. My footstep, as I shuffled inside, echoed. A large room, then. My curiosity piqued. Even though I could go upstairs now in a limited capacity, I'd yearned for so long to discover what lay behind these doors that this seemed a special miracle.

When I couldn't see anything in the darkness past the thin shaft of light left from the corridor, I wedged my shoes in the door to keep it from closing and ran back to my room barefoot to fetch a light. Armed with a lantern, I returned.

Inside were lines of narrow beds with sheet-covered forms lying on them. There must have been fifty of them at least. I lowered my lantern, afraid I would wake whoever these people were, if they were people. They didn't stir at all, except maybe the whisper of a breath. Gathering my courage, I moved further inside.

Sheets obscured the faces of the figures. Core tightening, I approached one that didn't seem to be moving or even breathing at all. I pinched the edge of the fine sheet and drew it down.

A dead face, eyes slitted open, haloed in long brown hair, met my gaze.

I recoiled, dropping the sheet. Were all these people dead? What was this place? Panicked, I clutched the lantern harder. Pulling back another sheet, I found another unconscious girl, but she didn't have the emptiness of death about her. It was difficult for me to tell, though.

Young woman after young woman lay on these deathbeds, unmoving. I compulsively unveiled an entire row. I couldn't stop. What if this was the fate allotted to me as well? I counted three who were certainly dead. The others seemed only to be sleeping, but none of them woke from either my light or footsteps.

My breathing came ragged as I rounded to the next row. These woman... Some of them looked familiar. My horror only grew with each unresponsive body I observed.

At the head of the next row was a white sheet slightly askew. The rest had been spookily uniform. I drew it back.

The lantern crashed to the ground in my shock. Hands over my mouth, I screamed. There on the bed, hands at her sides, braided hair laid over one shoulder, was Lizzie.

I shook my sister's shoulder. There was still some pink in her cheeks to suggest she was still alive, unlike some of the other young women in the crypt-like room.

"Lizzie!" I cried, my eyes full of tears. "Lizzie, wake up!"

She jiggled back and forth but didn't open her eyes.

Gasping back sobs, I kissed her cool forehead. "Lizzie…"

A flame caught the corner of my eye and I righted the lantern to keep it from setting the white sheets on fire.

My sister had been here, mere doors down from my prison room, the entire time? Sadness made way for rage.

"Stay here," I commanded in a shaky voice, laying a parting hand on Lizzie's shoulder.

Running back to my room, I fetched one of the healing potions I had already tried to use, unsuccessfully, to remove the marks on my shoulder. Unstoppering the bottle, I tipped its contents out onto my finger, drawing the liquid across Lizzie's forehead and dabbing it on both eyelids.

"Wake up," I whispered. "Lizzie, come back to me."

I stared at her still form, her familiar features, now devoid of the spirit I knew so well. Would she ever wake?

After a few minutes of nothing, I knelt by her bed, leaning my head against its hard corner. The night passed slowly in an aching haze.

Lizzie never woke.

IT BROKE MY HEART TO CLOSE THE DOOR BEHIND ME AS I emerged the next morning, groggy and heartsick and furious. Endymion had had my sister all along. He was poisoning or enchanting or killing all those beautiful young women from Selene. For what? Why would he want a room full of sleeping maidens? The possibilities chilled me. And some of them had undoubtedly been dead. Why not take them away and give them a proper burial ceremony?

I made more healing potions and tried them all on Lizzie, daubing them against her soft lips or holding them under her nose to inhale the scent, but nothing elicited so much as a flutter of her eyelids.

Finally, I napped properly in bed. I had no sense of time anymore and no desire to emerge onto the upper levels to find out.

"Still asleep?" inquired an amused voice.

Lip curling, I turned on my side to see Calyse holding the door open with one hand. He was back in his warrior leathers.

"I had a momentary break and thought I'd eat with you, but if you'd rather sleep..."

"No," I said hastily, rising. "Is Endymion back yet?" I asked the question as casually as I could, but Calyse could almost certainly sense the rage seething just below my words.

"He's due to return in a few hours."

"Oh." The syllable was breathless, anticipatory. When I had the King alone, I would make him pay for what he did to Lizzie. Someone else could win the war against Im Scathail. Endymion had let it drag on too long anyway.

"I'll meet you in there," he said, eyeing my slim black night-dress and closing the door.

Minutes later, I found the dining room. Immediately I scanned for silverware. My only reason for coming at all was to find—ah! There it was. A knife. My heart tripped fast as a hummingbird's as I took my customary place at the table. As usual, a sumptuous feast had been prepared, far more than was needed for two people.

I ate, spoke politely to Calyse, and stole the knife.

A few hours, he had said. In a few hours, Endymion would return from his vague errand and come within arm's reach of me.

I tried to seem casual, but my skin slicked with cold sweat and I was trembling by the time I left the dining room. "I've remem-bered something about the golden brush," I told Calyse, voice even, more or less. "I just need to check something, but I should know for sure by the time the King arrives. Please let him know."

With the image of my sister's face before my mind, I secured the hidden knife in my sleeve and returned to my room to wait.

If Calyse suspected anything because of my words or manner, he didn't show it, instead smiling easily as he opened the door for me. Alone, I tugged the knife from my sleeve and slid it through one of the leather straps in the back of my dress.

The next few hours felt like days. Perhaps it was a full day, and all I could think about was my beautiful sister, my best friend, dying in the next room. I don't know how I managed or what I did during that time.

A quiet tap outside my door signaled that someone was

coming. Usually, I didn't hear anyone approach, but my ears had strained so forcefully to sense Endymion's arrival that the sound hurtled my heartbeat into my throat. My fingers twitched toward the knife at my back, but no. I couldn't grasp it yet. The King had to come fully inside the room, get close enough to me that it would only take one swipe to get revenge for Lizzie.

No knock preceded the door swinging open on silent hinges. Dark leather encased his strong body and bright gold adorned his ears. I was struck by how large he was compared to me. He stood at least a head taller, and everything from the cut of his jaw to the evident muscles in his arms and chest told me I'd stand no chance in a physical fight unless I caught him by surprise. His light amber eyes found me at once. I felt conspicuous standing there in the middle of the floor, obviously doing nothing but waiting for him.

"You have information?" he asked without preamble.

"Yes," I said, my voice a little shaky. I wasn't the brave one. I was the cautious one, but I had to be brave enough for the two of us now. I cleared my throat. "Yes, I do."

His eyes narrowed. Did he suspect me? "What is it?"

"Over here," I said. "I've discovered the source of the golden brush." I headed to the fireplace at the foot of the large bed, careful not to turn my back to him.

After a heartbeat, Endymion stalked forward with all the grace of a predator. He surveyed the fireplace burning low after one of the attendants had lit in a few hours ago. The mortar and pestle sat at the edge of the hearth.

He was almost close enough to me now that I could feel the heat of him, smell the faint spice and moss scent of him.

I held my breath. The air pulled taut.

Then, with all the speed I could muster, I snatched the knife and swung it upward at the Fae King. A scream ripped from my throat as all my fury came pouring out. I barely inhabited my body, moving with necessity.

But my knife. It was gone. I glanced to see it clatter away across the wood and marble floor. The pinprick of a blade rested in the soft spot beneath my chin, forcing my face upward. Endymion gazed down at me, somehow fierce and calm at the same time. His supernatural eyes bored into mine. He had wrestled me, fast as thinking, against the wall by the fireplace, his knife and his body keeping me in place.

My throat bobbed with anger and panic, but the King simply regarded me, his focus shifting from my wide eyes to the rest of my face. Now the warm spice smell of him filled my senses. I couldn't escape. I'd threatened him. He was only playing with me like a cat with its supper.

When he bent closer, I flinched, and his knife pricked me just slightly. Seeming to realize it was still there, Endymion removed its pressure from my neck.

"I underestimated you," he whispered slowly, the sound like a deep rumble echoing in his chest. I felt its vibrations. "What have I done so terrible that you would plague me this way?"

"Lizzie," I choked.

"You talk about things you don't understand."

Heedless of danger, I shoved his hard chest. He stepped back. The knife in his hand glinted in the firelight. He didn't look worried so much as exasperated. Terrified but determined, I hurtled on. "You had her all along," I said, volume rising. "You've been keeping women here, drugging them... I don't know. They're dying. You lied to me!"

"Is that all?" he sheathed his knife, insolence returning.

I gaped at him. "Is that all?" I repeated incredulously. "You are a sickening monster if you think—"

"They all ate fairy fruit. Do you know what that does?" His

calm demeanor infuriated me even more. "Humans waste away. Oh, it's ecstatic at first, pleasure like they've never known. They crave it. They gorge themselves on it, sucking on every last drop."

His deep voice and his nearness, paired with his words, seemed suddenly indecent. My blood pulsed everywhere.

"But then," he continued slowly, "it's too much for them to handle. They burn from the inside, aging prematurely, spiking with pain and longing that cannot be satisfied. Nothing can retrieve them from the yearning they feel for more."

He was close now, glaring at me, nearly touching.

"I find them in the woods. They're unable to return home after their encounter, so I bring them here. I can't reverse the effects, but I can offer them whatever peace I am able. Sleep that allows them to remain young and pain-free is all I can give. So that is what I do. I didn't know your sister was among the maidens, but I suspected it."

"Can you wake her?"

"It would do no good. She would crave only fairy fruit. She wouldn't know you."

Grief rose up in a wave. Part of me still wanted to speak with her, to see if I could break through her craving until she saw me, her sister, who loved her. "Is there no way to save her?" I whispered.

"Curses cannot be broken until their creator is destroyed, and sometimes not even then."

"Who created the curse?" But I knew the answer before I'd finished asking the question.

"Im Scathail." He walked over to retrieve my fallen blade. Pressing it into my hand again, he said, "I suggest you let me do my work. Your existence is distracting enough without a knife at my throat."

He turned his back, utterly unconcerned about the danger I

posed. Before he left the room, he turned one last time. "I am sorry about your sister. If you do discover anything more about the golden brush, send an attendant to me with the message." His gaze dropped to the knife I held limply in my fist. My chest heaved with emotions I couldn't name. "Good night, you thorn in my side."

❧ 13 ❧

My fingers curled around the stoat handle, but the door didn't open today. I laid my forehead against the impassable wood and closed my eyes. "I love you," I breathed.

I would do anything for my sister, even if it meant giving up my own future so she could have one.

I couldn't believe what I was considering. Only the overwhelming love I had for Lizzie could tempt me to contemplate it.

But first, I had to be sure about the prophecy, and that meant finding the Oakmaiden. I needed to hear it from her own lips, not secondhand from another Fae.

When I returned to my room, the tallest attendant—I'd learned her name was Neoma—was letting out my dresses. Needle in hand, she stitched the back of the maroon gown as though she were playing an instrument. The combination of rich food and no hard labor in the garden had given me more shape than merely slender gristle.

"Welcome back," she said smoothly, although she must have seen my eyes were red from crying.

"Neoma."

The Fae lifted her elegant head. Her large eyes, ice blue, met mine.

"Do you know where I can find the Oakmaiden?"

"The Oakmaiden?" She sounded surprised. "Only great lords and ladies seek her out."

"I'd like to see her, if I can," I persisted. I felt as if the ground under me were dragging me forward and there was no way to stop. I had to see this through, even if I received answers that made me sick to think about.

"The Oakmaiden dwells in the center of Tylaith Castle," Neoma replied in her low, measured voice. "Its walls were raised around her."

That dizzying thought did little to settle my growing nerves. I remembered the tower Calyse had shown me. What was in the center of the castle? Even from that great height, I couldn't be sure that I'd seen the entire structure. Its size was too grand for me to contemplate properly. The biggest building I'd seen before my capture were three-story granaries, and those weren't meant for dwelling places but storage.

Not to mention, that meant the Oakmaiden was ancient, older even than many of the Fae, whose lives spanned hundreds of years at least.

"Thank you," I said distractedly, sprawling down on the deep blue coverlets to think. If only nobility consulted the Oakmaiden, would she speak to me? Neoma had been quick to offer guidance, so hopefully others would give me directions as well. I felt, however, that I should keep my quest secret from Calyse and certainly Endymion.

The other attendants would enter shortly for my bath. I wouldn't be able to leave until after that. Reaching for my book, I leafed through the pages, almost forgetting until the wretched marks appeared that Endymion had written on the book Lizzie had given me as a birthday present. I stuffed down my aggravation but couldn't help reading his notes on my work.

She should have helped him, read one note beside a fight between Orlando and a lion attacking his sheep. Strangely, I'd considered that very thing as I wrote this secretly in my room. Genevieve watched the fight in horror without attempting to aid her lover.

Moving on, I found another scrawled notation, this time a part that was underlined, not amended or scratched out. *Genevieve longed to live forever in his arms, their love a barrier against the evils of the world.*

I gazed at the line. It wasn't so bad. Other passages made me cringe to reread them, but not that one. Endymion had appreciated it too. That, or it stood out to him as nonsense. He'd made it perfectly clear that he didn't believe in love.

"Your bath is ready, miss."

True to form, the other two attendants had appeared as though they were secretly ghosts who could walk through walls.

I disrobed, walked into the water, and thought of Endymion's face so close to mine I could smell his breath against my mouth.

❧

I DONNED MY VEIL IN THE UPPER LEVELS, FEELING AWKWARD there alone, without Calyse to escort me. Surprisingly, everyone knew where the Oakmaiden dwelt and the people I asked weren't shy about pointing me in the right direction.

One Fae held a sleek bear on a leash. "She dwells through the Rose Room," she said with a reverent tilt of her neck.

I wondered how many visited this place. It couldn't be a great number of humans, I reasoned, because this was the Other Kingdom, the land through the barrier. Magic or something older prevented humans from seeing this enormous edifice rising above the trees. Legends told of seductively beautiful lands beyond the woods, but everyone agreed the journey was so treacherous that it was better to live one's life in ignorance than to attempt to see them.

After a bit of fumbling, I followed the Fae's instruction to the Rose Room. The colonnade I'd seen with Calyse was only one of several rooms of equal grandeur. I had to pass through two of them to find the Rose Room. The second was all river stone and waterfalls, thin and strong as twine, rippling from somewhere far above. The blue stone I'd seen peppered throughout the palace glowed out of the night dimness in that space as though lit from within.

Flanked by two armored Fae guards, a profusion of painted and metallic roses created a frieze against the far wall, spilling onto the door—red as bright as poppies and dark as spilled blood, fiery orange as Calyse's eyes, and pale yellow like a cloudy winter sun. Crystals dusted them all like dew. The beauty of the illusion stole my breath, making me suck in the thin veil.

It took me a moment to remember why I had come.

The guard on the left, a handsome, dark-skinned Fae who looked a little like Calyse but less muscled and taller, challenged me in a language I didn't understand.

Covered in confusion, I stammered, "I would like to see the Oakmaiden... hear the Oakmaiden repeat a prophecy."

The guard's gruff expression also wasn't one I'd ever seen on Calyse, who often smirked or, at worst, looked thoughtful. He switched to a language I could understand. "The oracle is not a sight to be gawked at."

"I'm not here to gawk," I replied, regaining my composure. "There is a specific prophecy I need to hear word for word. I respect her words too much to trust them secondhand."

The guard glanced at his counterpart, a red-haired male, who nodded back. "Very well." The Fae I'd spoken to stretched out an arm and opened the door wide for me to enter.

Feeling small, I crossed the threshold into a dim, windowless space. There were no other creatures, just long basins of water with real roses floating upon the surface stretching the length of the hall. The effect struck me as lightless fire.

I followed the only route I could, toward the end, where another, unguarded door lay in darkness. This I opened. Within was a circular room with intricate stone flooring. Gray and green moss grew up through the mortar and clung to the stone. The walls were porous with bookshelves and scrolls and writing implements. Two banks of simple tiered seating rose on either side of the room, facing a hole cut in the center. Arching out from the center hole came a tree as lovely as music. Its shape reminded me of a woman, contemplative and young, but with a soul as ancient as the sea. Bark obscured some of her features, but not enough to belie her beauty and strength.

I stood in front of the first row of seats and bowed my head. Her face was level with the third tier. "I hear you are the famous Oakmaiden." My words felt hollow and reedy, insufficient for communicating with a being such as this.

Her eyes did not turn to me, but the autumnal leaves above her rustled.

"Please, I would like to hear the prophecy about how marriage could end the war with Im Scathail."

A hiss like a breeze through leaves blew through the room at the enemy's name but the Oakmaiden still did not deign to move, if she could. When she spoke, would I even understand her? I hadn't understood the guard outside at first.

I hesitated before continuing. "I must know. And, I must

know if that would end his curse on fairy fruit and set all the people free who had suffered under his spell."

A cracking sound, like wood splintering, cut through the air. The ancient-youthful face looked down at me. "You have many questions, mortal girl." The Oakmaiden's voice was like a sigh, but felt richer in my ears, like a chant or a hearty wind through the forest. "My sight is long. My roots are deep, but they do not see all futures. One thing only will I give you."

Slowly, she lowered one upraised limb. Her gaze turned vacant and black as holes bored within her trunk. The temperature dropped and my ears popped as they did before storm.

I stepped back. The crook of my knees hit the bank of seats.

"King Endymion, monarch glorious of the Fae, battles the Shadow, enemy to all. A mortal girl steps amid the blood of both. If she would wed the King, all war against the Enemy will cease."

The Oakmaiden's commanding, otherworldly voice raised the hairs on my arms. Wind blew my veil and skirts.

Once she had finished, the room whirled into quiet again. I stood panting before the seer's placid form. She was once again a graceful tree. I did not expect any more conversation or clarification from her after that pronouncement.

If she would wed the King, all war against the Enemy will cease.

It was the confirmation I had sought. Relief and disappointment warred inside me. I didn't want it to be true, but I also wanted a clear step forward to helping Lizzie.

I had to marry Endymion.

It didn't matter that he was proud or cruel or that, despite his seductive allure, he believed love to be a harmful myth. It didn't matter that I hated him for what he had done to us. Marrying Endymion could help not only Lizzie, but also the Fae and, if he was right, everyone I'd ever known.

14

I tried to catch Endymion at breakfast to propose my plan to free Lizzie from her cursed sleep and end his war for good. The problem was that, even when he was in the castle, the King didn't often stay long, dropping by briefly and unannounced to chat with Calyse before leaving again. Even those short visits happened only once every other day or so.

It was three days before I saw him again. Regathering my nerve before each meal was beginning to wear on me. I didn't want to marry Endymion and he certainly didn't want to marry me, but I'd prepared my case. Hopefully, he would see reason.

I adjusted the gauzy pink gown to cover the bare minimum for modesty and exhaled slowly.

For Lizzie.

The diaphanous layers of the skirt frothed around me as I walked. Truthfully, I felt like a princess of story, perhaps Genevieve herself. Last night, I'd found another annotation by Endymion in the middle of my book. He'd crossed out the line I'd written about Genevieve choosing to run away with Orlando rather than follow through on her duty to marry the cruel prince of the neighboring land. Irritation—presumably at her choice to prefer love over duty—made the marks jagged.

I shuddered, but, throwing my shoulders back, headed to the dining room.

Conversation sounded through the door before I arrived. "At every turn," someone was saying. The deep, resonant voice sounded like Endymion.

"Would you prefer I keep her locked up like a dog?" Calyse. "End, you know she can't be a prisoner here forever. I was just trying to help her see us in a better light. You were doing a beautiful job painting us out as monsters."

"I can't afford to make us look like anything else, Cal."

"Forever melodramatic..." The words faded.

They sensed me.

Trying to control the anxiety I felt at interrupting, I opened the door and went inside. Endymion and Calyse sat adjacent to each other at one corner, Calyse occupying the spot at the head where Ellis sometimes sat. The King's radiant eyes raked over me, his full mouth set in a hard line. Perhaps he was inspecting me for weapons, but I'd left the knife I used to threaten him under the mattress. His attention felt sharp as any blade.

"Good morning!" Calyse exclaimed. "I hear you have been exploring the castle more. I think that's wonderful. Don't you, End?" He jabbed his friend in the side with an elbow.

The King grunted and cut a corner of fried, jam-covered bread with his knife and fork. His face looked somewhat gaunt in this light, its planes and edges sharper than before. His dark hair fell disheveled over his forehead. The bright golden eyes were ringed with bruised circles that reminded me of the shadows I'd seen curling from him like steam that one night in the library.

I sat across from him. "Are you... well, my lord?" I asked,

reaching for politeness, anything that could make him take my offer more seriously.

He looked up sharply, evaluatingly.

"He has these episodes," Calyse explained.

This pronouncement seemed to plunge Endymion into an even worse mood. "I'm leaving tomorrow."

"Again?" I asked. Where did he go so often? Was he fighting Im Scathail alone?

"Don't get in trouble while I'm gone." The slightest hint of a smirk sparkled, there and gone instantly.

Calyse appeared to notice it. "She has been a fine guest, given her restrictions. Not a soul aboveground knows about the markings, or we would have heard. I, for one, think it's lovely to have a human around."

The King huffed. Evidently, he hadn't shared with his friend that I'd tried to murder him.

Calyse pushed him. "Be grumpy, then!" Turning to me, he added, "He had a bad night."

I took a bite of syrupy biscuit without tasting it. "I'm sorry."

"I'll fix it," he muttered to himself, and stood.

"You're not going to stay?" Calyse asked.

"You know how many preparations I have to make, Cal. Enjoy the meal with your guest." He deliberately emphasized the last two words.

I pursed my lips, annoyed, but I couldn't let him leave, especially knowing he would be gone again for who knew how long. I wasn't sure if Lizzie could survive until he returned.

"Endymion!" I rose, setting the napkin beside my uneaten food. "May I talk to you?"

"Like last time?" he asked evenly.

"No..."

I sensed Calyse perk up.

"Well then?" The King waited for me to speak.

"I would... It would be better in private."

One of his eyebrows lifted. After a moment, he addressed Calyse. "Give us the room. Five minutes."

"You're sure five will be enough?" Calyse asked roguishly.

"Yes," came Endymion's sharp reply.

The other Fae left and, with him, any cheerfulness. I laced my fingers together to steady myself. The last time I was alone with Endymion, I'd tried to kill him. How different my purpose was now...

"I learned the entire prophecy that's on my arm," I began, business-like. I lowered the scarf I'd wrapped around myself to hide it.

The King's gaze lighted on the golden markings. "And?"

"I think we should marry. If it will end the war, I'm a mortal girl and you—"

But he was laughing.

"What?" I snapped.

"I wouldn't wish that fate on anyone," he said, his wide smile showing his canines, "even you."

His mocking dismissal of my sacrifice infuriated me. I was trying to do the right thing and he wouldn't consider it for a moment. "I don't *want* to marry you, but if it could save your people and save my sister, then I think we have to."

"Oh, you would enjoy it," he said, still clearly amused. A bolt of warmth shot through me at his surety. "But I would destroy you eventually."

"I'm... willing to take the risk."

His fiery gaze softened, almost with pity. "No."

I frowned. "Why are you like this?" I cried. "Don't you want the war to end?"

"More than you know."

"Then you don't believe the prophecy?"

"The Oakmaiden's words are always true, but they often don't mean what you think. Truth is not always simple."

"Can't we try?" A new idea struck me. "Would an engagement be enough to call a truce? You could announce it to the forest folk to make them stop stealing girls from the village, at least."

That made the King pause. "How long do you think an engagement could last? Your kind has far shorter memories than ours," he said slowly, not rejecting the idea but mulling it over.

My skin hummed with life. Perhaps this could work after all. "I don't know," I admitted. "But any time gained without kidnapping or bloodshed would count as a small victory."

He looked me over again, thinking. He ran his thumb over his bottom lip. "You're more persuasive than I would have reckoned, little thorn," he said at last. "I'll think it over while I'm gone. I make no promises, but perhaps this is an avenue worth trying after all."

"How long will you be away?" I persisted.

"As long as I must. Why? Will you miss the sight of me?"

He didn't give me time to answer before he smirked, a little sadly this time, and left the room.

❦ 15 ❦

I laid my palm against the stoat door on my way to the library. With Endymion gone, I didn't fear running into anyone there. Research and mixing charms from garden herbs kept my mind from dwelling on Lizzie or the sacrifice I'd agreed to make on her behalf. Most of the time, at least.

What would engagement to a Fae King look like? An announcement? No real change from the life I was living now? Or would there be a ceremony of some kind? Would we have to touch each other?

Questions bubbled and swirled like the water in my circle bath. I didn't know what to hope for, except that this nightmare would end and Lizzie and I could go home.

Something Endymion had said stuck with me. *You would enjoy it. But I would destroy you eventually.* What had he meant by that? A truly good king wouldn't expect to destroy their mate, but he had sounded so certain. My mind drifted too often to both claims—one frightening and the other more seductive than I wanted to admit to myself.

I don't have to marry him, I assured myself, pulling open the door to the library. *We only have to be engaged.*

Book smell wafted up, dusty and spicy with a hint of Endymion's scent. I set to work. Now that I knew the prophecy, I wanted to discover more about what Endymion had done to eliminate this threat, and what more, if anything, could be done. If our ruse didn't last, I wanted a backup plan.

A pamphlet wedged between two bound volumes read *Of the Great Sleep.* I lowered myself into the green armchair, letting its cushions embrace me.

The Great Sleep is a lamentable period of our recent history, when the Fae were cast into enchanted sleep for thirty years. Many lost their lands and some their lives in that period of helplessness.

I'd heard most of this before. I leafed past the initial description until my eyes snagged on a familiar name.

King Endymion labored to wake his kingdom with little result until the thirty years had passed. Some foul rumors allege he neglected to help the Fae at all, instead enjoying the fruit of their work with no one to visit repercussions upon him.

The King hadn't slept a hundred years ago? How had he escaped the curse that plunged the rest of his subjects into a sleep that sounded hauntingly like Lizzie's?

I jumped up from the chair, searching for a book of records I had found the week before, which outlined dates and noteworthy events in Fae history. Most of them were uninteresting or incomprehensible to me, but now I cross-referenced the years of the Great Sleep with Endymion's activities.

Unsurprisingly, few events took places in the thirty years of the curse. I shifted my attention to the dates just before. A trade agreement, a murdered noble, a holiday, a battle, a new addition to the castle... I didn't know what I was looking for, but something told me I was missing a connection somehow.

An engagement.

I stopped skimming.

King Endymion engaged to a mortal woman of great beauty by the name of Rose.

The next item claimed they had set a wedding date. There followed a gap of several weeks when neither Endymion nor his bride-to-be was seen.

Rose dies tragically. King Endymion refuses to address the Fae about the loss.

Several more days when the King was unaccounted for. Then the Great Sleep.

The timing of the Great Sleep coincided too closely to Rose's death to be a coincidence. And the fact that Endymion didn't sleep at all. What was he doing in those days following his lover's demise? And... how did she die?

I would destroy you eventually.

Something wasn't right here. I couldn't piece everything together, but the handsome Fae King wasn't innocent in all this. Either he had killed Rose, or his grief was so great that it spread across the Other Kingdom in a curse.

I circled my neck with my fingers, willing my pulse to slow. No, surely I was inventing falsehoods. These imaginings were the result of my fevered brain, apprehensive about finding myself in the same position as Rose. Perhaps she had merely died of a terrible accident and no foul play at all. Im Scathail retaliated after the prophecy had failed to come true. That was all.

But I couldn't shake the sense that I was missing something important. The speedy order of events suggested a link.

A few more hours of searching stirred no new connections, and my eyelids grew heavy. I closed the copy of *Royal Edicts and Strategies* I held on my lap and left to return to my room.

Mind roiling, I changed into the black silk nightdress and slid between the covers. The fire at the foot of the bed snapped and sizzled. With every sound, my thoughts skipped to new, terrible possibilities. Even without my feverish theories, marrying Endymion seemed like the only solution. Though I recoiled from it, I knew I ought to try again to convince him to do more than announce an engagement. Part of the trouble was that he had lived so long that it could take me until I withered and grayed to change his mind.

"Cal!"

The ragged shout cut through my thoughts. I bolted upright, the covers slipping from me.

"Cal!"

Though I'd never heard him use that desperate tone before, the voice was unmistakable. It was King Endymion.

"Where are you, damn it? Calyse! Cal, come out here!"

My insides chilled at the anguish in his voice. I crept from bed. Endymion must be just down the hallway. Was something happening to him? I heard no enemy. It was impossible to gauge exactly how far away he might be. Could he be outside the stoat room? That possibility sent me hurtling toward the door. If Lizzie were in more trouble...

Yanking open the door, I saw Endymion stumbling around the corner from the opposite end of the hall. Shadows completely enveloped him, far more than I'd seen in the library that day. He wore the dark leather he usually did, but it had been torn and he wore no gold in his ears. Grime caked his normally perfect skin. His eyes, wide and wild, had darkened from gilded fire to glossy black. They locked on mine.

I choked back a scream.

Barely able to keep upright, the King staggered toward me. "Help," he said, though what he thought I could do, I had no idea.

Releasing the door handle, which I'd been compulsively gripping, I hurried back to the hearth where I'd left some extra healing charms and potions. None of them had been potent enough to wake my sister or even to erase the marks on my arm, but I grabbed the clinking bottles and brought them to the door.

Endymion collapsed half in and half out of my room. In a panic, I rolled him onto his back. His eyes had closed and the darkness seethed around him so powerfully that I was having trouble making out his features in the murk.

"Here," I muttered nonsensically, "take this." It was the most basic healing charm I knew, the one I'd discussed with Lizzie days before she disappeared. I had no idea if charms would work at all on this side of the barrier, much less on a Fae instead of a human.

I poured the remains into his mouth, but his teeth were shut tight, as though he were in pain, so some of the liquid dribbled from his lips. I only waited a beat before trying another one, this one activated by scent. Still no response. I dabbed the last potion on his lips, spreading it across them and between.

Seemingly fueled by the King's helplessness, the shadows grew and multiplied. It was like working in the smoke of a burning house. The writhing shadows became creeping tendrils, then horrible faces, then hands reaching for me. At first, I thought my terror invented figures in the black mist, mirages, but then the fingers snagged on the strap of my nightdress and it fell off my shoulder.

I tripped backward in my haste to get away. Forms materialized out of the shadows, rolling toward me like fog, billowing from the King's prone body. Skeletal fingers stretched out, catching the hem of black silk. Their cold touch wrapped around my ankle, sinuous as a snake. I felt it now as a physical thing. The shadows would get into my mouth, my eyes...

"Cal!" I cried, unsure of anything else to do. "Neoma! Somebody, help!"

Horror rooted me in place as the shadows squeezed and grasped and threatened to consume me.

A shape rose near me from the darkness. I couldn't be sure who or what it was. Nothing in my life had prepared me for this. Unfamiliar words poured from the figure, deep and commanding.

At the sound, the shadows retreated slowly as though sucked back to their evil source. Bit by bit, the snake-like tendrils released me, dragging against my skin in a sickening farewell.

As gradual and quick as dawn—one moment far off and the next lighting the sky—the darkness subsided. In the heart of the shadows stood Endymion, still smoking gently like a candle.

I opened my mouth to thank him for whatever he had done to save me, but he wavered heavily and fell to a knee. His eyes, unfocused, still looked dark, but I saw gold in them again. All I could do was help him to the bed before he collapsed again.

This time, the shadows didn't multiply. Shivering in the cold—the fireplace had gone dark—I hugged myself in that torn nightdress, too shaken to make any sense of what I'd witnessed.

I was still standing there over Endymion's unconscious body when Calyse finally entered a few minutes later.

He didn't ask what had happened, almost as if he already knew. Instead, he cast me a concerned glance before rushing to the bed and checking to make sure the King still lived.

"I didn't do anything," I said weakly.

"I know." Calyse's untied shirt showed a large expanse of dark skin beneath. Perhaps the shouting had woken him. He bustled about Endymion's body, inspecting the King's clothes, hands, and face in a methodical manner that made me loose a shaky breath. At least someone seemed to know what to do.

After he was satisfied with his examination, he turned to me. "Are you all right? You must have gotten a fright." Before I answered, he added, "Nobody can hear about this. No one at all, do you understand?"

I could only nod. The fear I'd tried to suppress came boiling up. I thought I would cry.

Leaving the King for a moment, Calyse embraced me, holding me tightly against his chest. The tears welling below the surface spilled out.

For Lizzie. For myself. Even for Endymion.

The Fae held me immovably, like a wall to lean on. Once I'd collected myself, I asked, "What was that? What are those shadows?" I kept cheating looks at the King and the steaming darkness still blurring his form.

Calyse looked more serious than I'd ever seen him. "That is not a story for today, I'm afraid, and it's not my story to tell. I *can* say that you were lucky to escape." He set his big hands on my shoulders. "The danger has passed." A tick in his jaw seemed to add *for now*. "You should not have seen what you did. I know End will be sorry when he wakes."

"It wasn't his fault," I said.

Calyse quirked a brow. "So sure about that, are you?"

The encounter with the shadows had totally rid my thoughts of the doubts I had about the King's previous engagement, the Great Sleep, the harm he claimed would come to me. Perhaps I shouldn't be so quick to trust.

"Were you playing the goddamn flute again?"

We whirled to see Endymion still prone on the bed, but with eyes open, looking at us.

"You can't fault someone for having hobbies other than stabbing people," Calyse laughed, relief evident in every line of his body. He rushed to the King's side. I followed.

"I can if the result is this catastrophe. You knew I was due to return this evening."

"Your timing is often wrong by a few hours."

"Rarely."

I saw clear relief in Endymion's face as well, alongside myriad other emotions like disappointment. Bone-deep disappointment.

Calyse appeared to see it too. He leaned toward his friend. "Maybe the next time," he said in an undertone.

Endymion sighed, his face oddly beautiful, even though—perhaps especially because—he lay dirty and unkempt, wreathed in dying shadows, upon my silken blankets. His golden gaze shot to me, almost as though he'd forgotten me until that instant. He peered minutely from my blonde head to bare foot.

"It didn't hurt you?" he asked.

"No."

"Just gave her a scare," said Calyse.

"Good," he grunted.

"I think you... stopped the attack somehow," I added. That action, at least, deserved commendation, even if he was guilty of some of the atrocities I'd read about.

We three felt like co-conspirators, privy to this great secret that I didn't understand.

"I've made up my mind," said Endymion, turning his face toward the ceiling. "We will be engaged."

I was about to protest when I remembered that the scheme had originally been my idea. Darkness floated up from his body. In the dimness it looked like reaching fingers.

※ 16 ※

After the incident with the sentient shadows, I elected to sleep in a small adjacent room while Endymion rested in my bed. Calyse reminded me as he pocketed the key not to tell a soul about my experience, even the part about my new engagement to the King. Despite his normally jovial nature, a threat lay under his words. If I told anyone what I'd seen, I'd forfeit my life.

The next morning, utterly groggy, I emerged, swathed in a fluffy robe Calyse had kindly provided with the room. Breakfast was tea and exotic fruits and tureens of tomatoes topped with soft eggs. I ate them mechanically, vaguely guilty for not appreciating such wonderful food more. Mother would have loved the flaky rolls served with the tomato and eggs.

Calyse wasn't in the dining room. Ellis was, but she rarely spoke to me. I understood that I could come to breakfast as I pleased, so I did. I realized that a torn silk nightdress and robe weren't proper attire for meals—at least, I assumed they weren't, since all the Fae dressed magnificently whenever they were out in public. The shock of the night before had dulled my capacity for self-consciousness.

That was, until Endymion appeared.

Endymion entered for breakfast, more resplendent that I'd ever seen him. No shadows curled around him now. He had washed and appeared completely unhurt. Even the dark rings around his eyes had gone. Today, in addition to the golden ear ornaments that ended in a point at the top, he wore a thin golden crown with delicate golden chains hanging from it, looping over his forehead and through his hair. His dark suit fit him perfectly, this time embellished with a golden tree that reminded me of the Oakmaiden. The embroidered design began at his hip and grew upward along that side and sleeve until the topmost leaves reached his collar.

He looked ancient and young all at once. If I hadn't seen him buckle to the ground the night before, I would have thought him undefeatable, a lesser god capable of beautiful and terrible things.

My heart jumped when he focused on me. "Are you going to look like that when we announce our engagement?"

My awe turned into annoyance. "You were using my room last night," I reminded him. "I haven't had the chance to change."

"Engagement?" Ellis cracked the word like a whip.

"Between me and Laura," he said, as though that were the most natural thing in the world. To my ears, however, his declaration sounded foreign. It stuck to me like the juice of fairy fruit, tempting and forbidden and cursed.

"There cannot be an engagement."

Endymion ladled himself a portion from the tureen. "There is."

His serene countenance exuded complete control. How many others knew of the darkness that possessed him? Did Ellis?

I stayed silent.

Ellis glared. I had seen her look vexed, bored, amused, and preoccupied, but never angry. Now she had blades in her stare. Her apparent age did nothing to mute the ferocity of that look.

Endymion did not respond. He bit into a roll with utter calm. As usual, he didn't stay long. Minutes of frosty silence later, he rose from the table. "Get dressed," he told me. "I'd like to start right away."

CHAFING FROM THE KING'S CARELESS AUTHORITARIAN MANNER and afraid of facing the choice I'd made to betroth myself to him, I returned to my room. The blankets had been snarled in the center where Endymion had lain. Smudges of dirt and what looked like blood smeared the top. I cringed. He had been bleeding? In my terror at the shadows, I hadn't noticed. At breakfast today he appeared as strong as ever, ethereally handsome and self-possessed.

I sighed and found that yet more clothes had materialized in the wardrobe. I had no idea that a single woman could own so many fine things, if indeed they were mine. Besides a replacement for my torn silk shift, one new addition in particular caught my eye, the fire-red of leaves at the peak of autumn. Its train flowed so long it pooled at the bottom of the wardrobe like blood. I drew it out. It had long sheer sleeves and a plunging neckline. Golden accents inlaid with tiny red stones burst like stars across the skirt and bodice. Boning in the corset supported its high collar, a spray of deep red fading into russet orange and finally, of course, gold.

It was a queen's dress. Beyond its finery, the style of it made me blush. I already drew too much attention with my mask aboveground. Although my daily baths with the attendants made me less embarrassed to show my body, the transparent pink layers of the second most revealing dress had made me glad not to have seen more people. Endymion's gaze alone had burned a blush into my skin.

A tiny click made me turn around. Neoma entered. She nodded at the dress in my hands, totally unsurprised to see me holding it. I felt again as though I'd been caught stealing.

"That is the one His Majesty wishes you to wear."

"What, this?" Instead of handing it to the Fae girl, I replaced it on its hanger.

The two other attendants entered behind her. I submitted to my bath and had to admit I'd grown to anticipate their ministrations and scrubbings and oils. I began absently to braid my long hair over my shoulder.

Neoma stayed my hand. "No."

I frowned. Was this also a preference of the King? If such a simple thing could aid in the illusion that we planned to wed, thereby ending the war and the curse, I'd comply. But this small act of control fell into a list of things I didn't like or trust about Endymion. He had saved me from the shadows but he had also released them on me, so that wasn't enough to save his reputation in my eyes.

Whenever I saw him next, I'd be sure to braid my hair.

The attendants put the fire-red dress on me. It squeezed my ribcage and swelled my breasts into outline. I wore my hair long on either shoulder because it couldn't fall down my back with the flamboyant collar in the way. The dress's train was as long as I was tall, suggesting tree shadows across the silky fabric, which I hadn't noticed before.

Something shiny glinted in Neoma's palm. My insides twisted when I saw what it was. Golden ear cuffs, intricate and pointed. She fitted them on the shell of each ear.

In that room, I felt like a queen. Never before had I felt so magnificent, freckles across my chest and all.

It was the idea of leaving the room that scared me. This moment might be pretend, some dream I'd wake up from and tell Lizzie. But if I left, if I saw Endymion in all his own magnificence, then I couldn't pretend any longer.

All in their own ways, Lizzie and Mother and Grandmother and Great-grandmother had told me to live rightly and to own my choices. They told me they loved me.

For them, I would own my choice now.

When the attendants opened the door, Endymion stood there as though he'd known exactly when to anticipate me. His gaze, somehow refined and sultry at once, raked over my body. My heart beat in my throat. I hated that his piercing attention made my blood respond. He was still my captor, no matter how alluring his form. I clenched my teeth. Today, I had to pretend to enjoy his presence.

The King's mouth twitched—a concession, I gathered, to how beautiful I looked. He offered me his arm.

I took it, steeling myself and trying not to notice the hard muscle beneath the pressed black suit. We matched perfectly, a symphony of the Oakmaiden's leaves and black and gold royalty.

"I've decided to waste no time," he said, voice low so no one else could hear, if anyone else had been with us in the corridor.

My breaths came shallow, nervous in such an avalanche of large and a flurry of small ways.

"You're pale," he observed.

I met his gaze, piercing and beautiful despite the darkness lurking within. "Yes," I said simply.

"It won't affect our plans, but I'd prefer if my subjects didn't think I coerced you. Cal reports that most already find me distant and harsh. All the better."

"I'm not... marrying you out of a sense of... love," I managed, struggling to get air. My revealing bodice was not the culprit, though it didn't help either.

"I'm not marrying you at all."

With that, we mounted the stairs. I took care to avoid tripping on my long dress.

At the top, sun burst through the high skylit ceiling, blinding me. Roaring applause shook the building and rattled my bones. I was nightmarishly on display before a huge segment of Endymion's kingdom. I wanted to cringe away from the frenzied screaming of the crowd, as though all was made right that had ever been wrong.

Still dazed, I felt the King shift beside me and slide his hand into mine. Tingling webbed up my arm at the sensation. He had calluses like I did, but his fingers felt warm and sure. Despite everything, in that dreamlike moment, his strong presence comforted me.

My eyes adjusted and I saw a gathering of thousands, Fae and forest creatures and exotic animals and men with goblin faces. They all stared, elegant in their own ways, whether long-limbed or goat-legged. A pair in front had beetle iridescence rippling through their faces like scales.

An edge of awe permeated the crowd, fear and exhilaration mingling into a manic excitement.

Endymion squeezed my hand. "I have chosen for my bride Laura of Selene," he declared, his deep voice resonating throughout the space.

A sense of unreality continued to plague me. How could he have organized the announcement this quickly?

"We will have a feast in her honor." He paused, the tiniest hesitation. Had his finger not twitched slightly, I wouldn't have noticed it. "My hope is that this union brings an end to long war!"

Another raucous, ear-splitting cheer.

The King descended from his exposed position atop the stairwell into the cavernous great hall. People and creatures made way for us, even avoiding my train.

A throne was brought out and set before one of the great trees on the far left side. Endymion approached and sprawled out in it, looking every inch the dissolute king of fairy tales.

"Sit with me," he said. "We'll be here a while." His expression was inscrutable.

I wavered, unsure. "How long?" I asked.

"These occasions last for days. Wine flowing, no one sleeps…" His eyes swept over the milling Fae. Tables and drink seemed to have emerged spontaneously into existence. "Trust me. I thought it best to begin, like I said, as soon as possible."

The throne was large but had no room for two. I swiveled to search out another option.

Endymion held out his hand, beckoning me forward, a wicked glint now clear in his eye. He thought this situation humorous.

"My lord…"

"You, my future bride, may call me Endymion." He leaned forward and, because he was so tall and I so close, he spoke the next words in my gold-encased ear. "We must make them believe."

He smiled, cat-like. He was infuriating.

"Is that how the curse works?" I whispered back, wanting to make sure he knew I took no pleasure in flirting with him.

"*You* asked *me* for this," he said, his voice dipping even lower, hardly a rumble, but I felt it in my chest.

I let him draw me forward and settle me on his lap. The train of my dress fanned out in front of the throne like an enormous rose petal. I straightened, trying not to lean against him too heavily but the position became uncomfortable quickly.

Endymion snaked an arm around my waist with a look so self-satisfied I could do nothing but scowl back at him.

"Belief," he said again, quietly enough that I could hear but none of the revelers could.

I adjusted myself and lounged, matching his position. The most comfortable spot was straddling his large thigh. The indecency of the position made me cringe, but he merely held me in place against his chest with one strong arm. Despite my outward ease, inwardly I was mortified. I didn't want to be comfortable. I didn't want to like this—wearing a queenly dress so form-enhancing that it must have been easy to picture off, and sitting on the lap of the Fae King in front of all his subjects.

But I did.

"This can't be so bad." His insistence on whispering must have given the impression that we were lovers speaking sweet or naughty things to each other.

I didn't reply. Happily, a creature with tall cupped ears like a doe tripped forward on tiny hooved feet. She reminded me of the fawn boy, so brutally killed by the King. My resolve hardened to distance myself from his attentions as soon as this party was over.

"By the shards," she warbled. "Your Majesty, what a handsome couple you make! Divine, for a mortal girl."

I took this dubious compliment with a smile. I couldn't resist the role I had to play any longer. So, I would play it and immediately afterward sit alone in my room. I would take a bath and read.

Yes, that sounded delicious. It would be my reward for acting, which went against all my natural personality. I was quiet, modest, obedient. In this place, though I was my family's only advocate and this my only avenue to success.

"Lady Springfell," the King muttered by way of response.

The doe-creature moved on, glossy eyes wide as though she couldn't believe her boldness in approaching us.

Wine appeared in Endymion's hand. He handed the glass to me and then got another for himself. I sipped mine immediately, the sharp warmth of the mulled flavors coating my mouth. It was morning, but everything the last few days had been topsy-turvy. I groaned in pleasure at the taste.

The next few hours passed in a blur of well-wishers and Fae nobles, wine and delicacies. I grew surer of myself by the minute, though that could have been the wine. I certainly felt flushed by it. Endymion's thumb stroked the very bottom of my plunging neckline, which ended at my midriff just above my navel, softly teasing the skin there when his thumb slipped up too far. I didn't mind it.

Dancing broke out in the evening. I had never seen such a spectacle. As the light faded, flames innumerable as stars fanned into the air, glowing in every corner. Fae lords and ladies ethereally beautiful, dressed in the finest clothes, moved with such strength and grace across the floor. I could practice for a lifetime and never look as stunning.

Beneath me, the King shifted. I blinked and turned to him. My heart plummeted in surprise at how much he exceeded those I'd been watching. Wine, perhaps, had turned him magnificent. Lamps like starlight lit his bronzed cheeks and did indecent things to his lips. How strange that he should be looking at me and not one of the Fae on the dance floor. I felt his arm around me anew, how sturdy it had been, adjusting me to more comfortable positions as though I weighed nothing.

"We should dance," he said. "I can show you if you don't know the steps. Or are you hopeless at such things?" His tone said he wouldn't be surprised.

"Maybe I am. I don't know." Sudden, drink-fueled courage prompted me to add, "But I'd like to."

To my surprise, he rose and immediately bent to gather the folds of my dress from the floor.

"What—?"

Instead of answering, he gripped my wrist gently and hooked a tiny clasp linking it to my train. The pressure of his fingers remained on the inside of my wrist for a moment longer. The flowing red skirt no longer dragged behind me, inhibiting my movements, but hung from my sleeve like a curtain.

I twirled, admiring the fabric's movement. "I didn't know it could do that," I said, very close to him. Apparently, my time in the throne had broken down my normal inhibitions about approaching him. I eyed his shoulder, which was at my eye level, trying to focus through the haze over my mind. No shadows. I dusted off his broad jacket as if to make sure.

"Now we are both ready," he declared with a smirk, not hiding the way he was looking at me.

Together, we parted the dancers until we stood in the center of the floor. Our very footsteps echoed back at us from the glass dome in the roof. We were inside and outside at once on a warm summer night when I could pretend nothing terrible had happened.

The music eddied around us, insistent and exploratory, a little like the music I'd heard in the forest when I'd found the feast in the hollow. I didn't understand how to dance to it. The revel in the barn hadn't required choreographed movements. Though chaotic, the dancers' movements here held such agility and precision that I had to suppose they were deliberate steps.

Suddenly unsure, I looked up at Endymion. He took my fingers in his and guided his other hand around my hip until it settled in the small of my back, pressing me to him. My breath caught at his warmth and surety and the knowledge that I wanted to press myself close to him.

He began to move. I wrapped my arm around his body to hold on. My head barely rose to his shoulder, so my entire view became his dark lapels and the tips of gold threading and the tan skin of his neck. I wondered what it felt like. His fingers were callused but his neck would be soft. I let the music take me as it had in the barn and in the woods. He whirled slowly, stepping with finesse that let me follow without fear of tripping. In my periphery burned a thousand little lights. The other dancers made way for us, opening a wide swath as we glided together, the Fae King and his betrothed. The scent of moss and heady spices made me dizzy with desire.

He slowed and dipped me backward, bringing his face to mine. I felt him exhale, the warmth feathering against my lips. His half-lidded expression held a hundred forbidden ideas. He remained there, gazing, holding me with the tautness of surprise or expectation. His face moved closer. I parted my lips...

But he righted me again to smattered applause. I didn't let go. Now that the idea had taken hold, I wanted that kiss. I'd touched his lips with my finger when administering the healing charms. I'd slid one inside his mouth to let the potion reach his tongue.

Emboldened, I turned my face up to his. The heat of his skin warmed my already blushing cheeks.

A finger hooked my chin before my lips touched his. He remained tantalizingly close, almost touching. I could lunge and get that kiss, but I knew even in my drunken lust that I didn't want to do it that way.

He met my eyes, the gold from his delicate crown matching the gold in his irises. He was painfully beautiful. His finger held my chin lifted so I could see him but not reach him. It was a sweet kind of torture.

"You've been drinking, little thorn," he said in the quiet voice we'd used before to speak privately. "Best not to get carried away."

"End," I gasped. The shock of using the King's nickname worked as well as frigid water to bring me to my senses. I straightened, stepped back, aware now of the haze that had settled on me, the blurred edges of reality that tempted me closer to Endymion.

"I have to leave anyway," he said, raising his voice to the normal volume. The dome magnified the words. A few more Fae and forest creatures looked at us.

"What? Leave?" I felt newly stupid and ashamed.

"You haven't asked about Cal," he observed, placing his palm on my back to lead me off the dance floor. "He's completing the preparations."

My shame doubled that I hadn't noticed the absence of one of my only friends.

I realized Endymion was leading us toward the stairs. "You're not staying for the rest of the party?" I asked.

He halted at the spot where he had announced us before, at the top of the descending staircase, a conspicuous place where all were sure to see us. Facing me, he curled a lock of hair around my ear before leaning to speak into it. My body still longed for that kiss and I melted a little at the contact. The mix of spices wafted up from his hair and the cool metal of his ear cuff touched my cheek.

"I have to make the most of time. We've announced our grand plans and now every hour is precious. Over time, they might suspect the truth, so I'm leaving tonight. The sooner I free the kingdom, the sooner we can... undeceive everyone. They won't be surprised we left early."

I flushed at the implication. Everyone believed us. Confusion covered me when I realized how proud I was to be linked to the King this way, for everyone to think we were lovers.

As though sensing my thought, Endymion gave a small, roguish smile and offered me his hand. We descended the steps. As soon as we reached the corridor at the bottom and closed the door behind us, he let go. The sound of revelry muted to a hush down here.

"Good night, little thorn," he said as he walked away in the opposite direction from my room.

🐾 17 🐾

The sheets had been changed in my absence. No sign of Endymion's struggle with the shadows remained. I stayed in bed late the next day, muzzy from the drinks at the party.

My betrothal party.

Memories came back in pieces, but sharply, with no ambiguity. I buried my face in the pillow when I recalled how desperately I'd wanted to kiss the King, to nip at his neck, to feel his tongue urge against my closed lips. The memory came back with such force that I had to force down residual desire.

That desire died when I saw my book was missing. Finally leaping out of bed, I tripped over to the little table where I kept it. *Tales of Orlando and Genevieve* wasn't tilted against the side or underneath the bed. I searched everywhere I could think of, including the wardrobe. The book had vanished.

No one would have thrown that book away and no one *else* would take it without permission. I ground my teeth. Endymion somehow had my book.

Why could he possibly want it? His mysterious missions

couldn't require it. And what were those missions? They related to the war, but how? If his trip this time had been a battle of some kind, he wouldn't have gone alone. His subjects didn't know about the shadows, so that meant he didn't bring many with him on these secret journeys. He did, however, bring my large book, it seemed.

My curiosity and annoyance burned by the time the attendants came in. They offered me their congratulations on my engagement. I tried to smile, but only managed a grimace.

Once in the circular bath, I asked Neoma, "Is the King gone this morning?"

"His Majesty left last night."

"Did he say where he was going?" I realized this information might be something I, as his betrothed, ought to know, but I pressed on. "Or did he say when he'd return?"

"Not to worry," he replied, running a sponge down my back. "The King is rarely gone long."

What that meant in terms of Fae lifetimes, I didn't know. "Not long" could mean a year.

"I am glad he has found someone again that he can love," one of the other attendants commented.

"Yes. Soon the war will end. We'll all be free," I said. Already, word was spreading outside the palace that the prophecy needed no more sacrificed maidens. The young women of Selene could live in peace. I rallied, glad for the reminder of why I had proposed this otherwise foolish plan. I didn't trust myself when I was with the King. As long as I was careful, this ruse would continue to help those I cared about.

"And the King has not been happy," Neoma added wistfully. "He has kept to himself ever since the Great Sleep."

"You were there?" I asked. They looked too young to have lived over a century ago, but then, so did Endymion. Hungry for answers now that this unexpected avenue had opened wide, I continued. My suspicions felt somewhat flimsy in the light of day, but I still didn't know what had happened to Endymion's previous lover and what connection their betrothal had to the Great Sleep that had almost wiped out the Fae. "What happened?"

Lines appeared on their smooth faces. "Sleep does strange things with time," Neoma began.

The others were so reticent in their words that they merely continued to wash my body and blonde hair, agreeing with their expressions.

"Waking was the worst part, finding one's body wasted, but we are rebuilding ourselves."

Still rebuilding after one hundred years. The thought staggered me. "What caused it, if you don't mind my asking?" This was the part I truly wanted to hear.

"Im Scathail," she replied automatically. "The Shadow."

The word made me prick up my ears. "It was a shadow?"

The hands and sponges paused as one, the attendant's eyes all becoming distant with horror and memory.

"I'm sorry..." I said.

"It was a shadow, a great, billowing cloud like black smoke." Neoma's cadence had become like a chant or a poem. "It reached over Tylaith Castle, smothering the windows, and it was within, grasping at our feet as we tried to run. But it caught even the quickest among us, pulling us down and pouring down our throats." She cut herself off abruptly with a shaky breath.

I put a hand on her shoulder. A slight tremor shook the Fae girl.

Her attention focused on me once more. "The King escaped. By the shards, we all thought he might have been... But he was alive when we found him, simply more serious. Quick to sadness, quick to anger, and now"—she placed her hand on mine—"quick to joy."

My brow knitted low. *Grasping shadows... The King escaped...* My theory fit too neatly with the facts. Besides, Endymion had told me himself that he put the captured maidens into an enchanted sleep, which he didn't even need the shadows to accomplish. I didn't want to ask more and risk any more pain to the attendants, who obviously hated and feared the memory.

Endymion and Calyse had both warned me strenuously about saying nothing to the others about seeing the shadows. Was this the reason? Could Endymion have caused so much terror among his own subjects? Something deep within me knew the answer.

I thought of the horror in the King's own face as he stumbled toward my room. He hadn't meant to send the skeletal shadows after me, but he had done it nevertheless. Was remorse enough to rid him of this historic sin—causing the Great Sleep? And what had happened to his beloved at the same time? Had he accidentally killed her too?

Totally unsettled, I passed the rest of my time in the pool in silence.

❧

Now, as Endymion's bride-to-be, I could wander to any part of the castle I chose without a mask. I still covered the golden markings on my arms out of habit and because no one had told me I could reveal them. Even with this newfound freedom, I often found myself in my room or in the dim downstairs library tracking down answers to the mysteries that plagued me. I was running out of books written in a language I could understand. Many more volumes lined the dark shelves, but their symbols were as opaque to me as the charm Lizzie had written on my arm.

I discovered nothing more. Neoma and the other attendants never brought up their traumatic past again and even Calyse, who hadn't traveled with Endymion this time, remained tight-lipped whenever I drew near the subject of the Great Sleep, the King's solo missions, or his long-lost beloved.

Unable to sleep one night, I padded down the familiar path to the library, touching the stoat door knocker as I passed it. Lizzie's door hadn't opened since I found her sleeping there. How much longer could she last if someone didn't break Im Scathail's curse?

My head felt heavy with secrets.

I pulled up short when I saw Endymion sitting in the green armchair. Déjà vu rocked me as I noticed the tiny curling steam of darkness rising from his shoulders. A line creased the spot between his brows. His hair looked messy, a far cry from the immaculate royal I'd witnessed just days before at the dance. Fatigue made him look older and younger at the same time, somehow.

He looked up at me wearily. "Are you going to interrupt me every time?"

"I didn't know you were back." I remained by the door.

"I don't announce it through the castle." Apparently, these trips of his put him in a grumpy mood.

I felt cross myself. "Perhaps you should announce it to me if you don't want me interrupting you in the library. I've been told I can come here if I like."

Once again, I'd surprised him in the library. Once again, I wore only the black nightgown supplied in the wardrobe. My apprehension was different this time, though. Seeing him again brought back both the decadent sensations from the party and all my doubts about his character.

The darkness wreathing around him unsettled me. He seemed to notice I was looking.

"They're not dangerous tonight," he said, languidly running his fingers through the air. Shadows puffed like an afterimage between them. "I know when they're dangerous."

Then I noticed a book on the shelf near him. "That's my book!" I exclaimed, going to retrieve it. I saw no ghostly fingers in the shadows this time, so I tried to ignore them as I approached. Unexpected emotion welled inside me as I clasped the book again. This was my sister's only memento for me and he had taken it. "Why did you steal it? Why did you *write* in it?" I demanded. My eyes prickled.

"The first time or the second?"

His question took me by surprise. "Both."

He sat back slowly in the chair as if his very bones pained him. Sitting on his lap as I had done at the party would hurt him now.

When the silence drew out, thin and taut, I decided other questions were better worth asking. "Where do you go when you leave like this? Do you face Im Scathail alone?"

"In a way."

It wasn't an answer. I adjusted the big book across my chest. Drawing in a breath, I gathered my courage for the next question. It was possible, I realized, that this one could land me in far more trouble than any other comment or accusation I'd made before, including the time I tried to stab him.

"You caused the Great Sleep, didn't you?" My voice was small but level.

His eyebrows shot downward. "Where did you hear that?" The authority in his tone returned, strong as it had been in the woods when we'd first encountered each other.

"Nowhere. Nobody told me."

"Have you blabbed your theory to anyone else?"

I disliked the accusation. "No, I haven't," I answered, glaring. "Did you?"

But his reaction seemed answer enough.

"You don't understand the whole story," he said, rising from the chair. "I don't even know how you came up with that idea."

"Reading."

He scowled at the books as though they'd wronged him. "You know... more than you should." I felt a warning in his words.

Straightening my spine and hugging my sister's book for reassurance, I returned his blazing look. "I know, but someone deserves to know. If you caused the Great Sleep, your subjects ought to—"

"They can never know."

"Is that because you killed your bride?"

His breath stalled. He looked utterly stricken. Running his long fingers roughly through his hair, he let out a humorless bark of a laugh. Darkness swirled around him. "Is that what you think?"

I wasn't sure I did, but the possibility pursued me relentlessly everywhere I went, just behind every innocuous thought.

I would destroy you eventually.

"The timeline suggests it. Even your own words suggest it. You can't love."

Muscles moved in his throat. I knew I'd doomed myself then.

"I may be a wicked king," he rasped, setting his golden stare on me, "but I have never met someone so determined to hate me."

He flexed his jaw and leaned against the table in the center of the room with one hand, his head dropping. "I didn't mean to harm any of them. And no, I don't intend to weave my tragic tale." Rallying, he stepped toward me again. "How is it that one day you long for me to ravish you in a room full of the strangers and the next you accuse me of atrocities so terrible you should fear to be alone with me?"

He stood so close now that the odor of spicy woods permeated the air around me. My pulse thundered in my ears. I wanted to ask why, why he had done such a thing, but the words became trapped in my throat. Fear crept under my skin at his power, but, if only because he needed me, I doubted he would hurt me. I glanced at the swelling muscles under his thin shirt.

He released a breath through his nose and gave me space to move. I did, walking to the door.

"You don't know what you think you do," he said to my back. "These shadows..."

I turned. He was chewing his bottom lip.

"They're... part of a curse. Calyse knows. And my mother. I already tried to fulfill the prophecy once. I will never do it again. Better to leave and defeat the Shadow myself, rid myself of these shadows than fall into the goddamn prophecy's trap again." These revelations came out in a monotonous rumble, as though these words echoed again and again and again inside him with little chance of release.

I hardly knew where to begin.

"You said the prophecy was true, that it would work," I said breathlessly. Our ruse still meant that maidens wouldn't be stolen from the forest, but if this was only a temporary solution and Im Scathail knew it couldn't actually end his reign of terror... My mind spun in circles.

"It did work," he growled, lip curling. "There's more than one way to end a war." He gestured as though directing music or performing a spell. The shadows trailed after.

I fought to keep up.

He let out a breath through his teeth. Whether he knew I wouldn't give up until I had answers or he was simply weak from whatever he did on his journeys, I don't know, but he continued. "You said I can't love. The opposite is true. Among the Fae, love, when we encounter it, is all-consuming. It's an obsession, a flame that won't burn out. Our very souls are knit together."

His golden eyes blazed and air pumped through him as though he had just finished a run.

"Rose was her name."

My stomach gave a jolt. So it was true. He did plan to marry, thereby ending the war. I recalled the lovely Rose Room leading to the Oakmaiden, shocked at myself for not making the connection sooner.

"What happened to her?" I whispered.

His wild expression frightened me with its desperation now. "She died," he said simply. "The prophecy wasn't fulfilled by marriage alone, but sacrifice. We didn't know until it was too late. My heart... My grief... The blood fueled enough dark magic to curse my dead heart, for the Enemy to... enter me like a disease."

He lifted his head with weighty significance and regarded me a moment as if resolving to tell me the damning truth. I held my breath, a lump in my throat. I feared to guess what might come next.

His next words were hoarse and slow. "I am the Shadow."

❦ 18 ❦

Horror washed through me. This was worse than my most terrible imaginings. Never in all the accusations I had thought or hurled at Endymion could I have guessed that he was Im Scathail.

He locked me in place with his eyes, glowing like a live fire in the dimness of the library. Silence smothered us, as though the first to move would have to acknowledge the ramifications of what he'd just told me. I couldn't face them, holding my book shield-like before me.

The King swallowed and broke our eye contact.

I flinched.

Now that I knew, how could I be allowed to live with this secret?

"You see why I can't marry you," he seethed, glaring at the rug.

Our betrothal had fled from my mind. His leap to that idea nearly brought a hysterical laugh to my lips.

"The Enemy would rip you to pieces. The war would end because there would be no resistance. The Shadow would control everything, even your little human town."

I still couldn't speak. My limbs trembled with too many emotions.

"Say nothing," he said, with the slowness and power of an immortal.

I shook my head, agreeing. "Is that," I gasped, "is that why you go? To free yourself?"

Something in his expression suggested that he hadn't expected me to stay, but to run. He was softer, somehow. "Possession doesn't end peacefully, it seems."

"Does he hurt you?"

He flattened his full mouth before answering, eyes once again revealing surprise. "Yes."

"How can I help you?" The words astonished me as much as they did him. When had my horror transformed into compassion? Was it even right to make this offer to a monster?

Slowly, he moved toward me. I did not retreat against the closed door. "You're helping me already," he said, leaving a just-respectful distance between us. "This agreement we've come to, it buys me time to seek out... remedies."

I remembered the dark circles under his eyes, the pain in his face when he'd collapsed in my room, the blood on the blanket. These solutions took their toll.

He tapped the cover of my book with a finger. "I skipped the end this time. It was better without it."

Blood pumping hard, I gazed up at him. Neither of us moved to leave.

More impulsive than deciding to go to the full moon dance, more impulsive than charging into the woods, more impulsive even than sitting on the King's lap in his throne was my next decision. I rose on my tiptoes and pressed my lips to his cheek.

I didn't—couldn't—wait to see his reaction, so I turned and fled.

SO MANY COMMENTS AND CIRCUMSTANCES FIT TOGETHER around the night's revelations that I felt I could finally make sense of the picture. What I couldn't make sense of was my own reaction. Endymion had told me he was responsible for the terrifying Great Sleep, that he was in some way part of Im Scathail, or that Im Scathail was part of him, and I felt more settled than I had before.

The truth was ugly, but it was real.

My role in helping him rid himself of the shadows ensured my safety for now, but, honestly, I didn't think I would fear even without that confirmation. I had surprised myself with boldness, but I hadn't been afraid when I'd kissed him on the cheek.

Lying in bed, I opened my precious book. The King's scrawls still wrecked the integrity of the margins and whole sections had been crossed out. A familiar pang of annoyance lanced through me, but I looked at the writing with a different eye. Endymion hated tragedy because he was living one. His love had been killed —Rose, the object of his obsession and desire, whose soul had knit to his.

I bit my bottom lip. He hadn't followed me out of the library.

A distraction. I needed a distraction. A few stories, I remembered, little things, hadn't been touched. I flipped to those.

Reading my own work had a double edge of fascination and embarrassment. I liked these characters but bemoaned my own inability to give them life. Right now, I wanted to lose myself in a fantastical world.

A dry chuckle escaped when I realized that my own situation would have fit perfectly within the confines of Orlando and Genevieve's world. What would they have done in my place? Surely something more valiant.

New writing inked the pages. This story told about the couple being attacked by wolves in the forest. After Orlando gets grievously injured, Genevieve tends to his wounds with the help of a woodland witch and, later, the pair share an amorous night in the forest.

It was a story I'd only shown to Lizzie, one I'd been a little ashamed to write, but that I liked to revisit. It took me on adventures and into passionate affairs I never anticipated experiencing in my real life.

Why so much violence? read one note next to the savage wolf attack.

I had gotten a bit overly descriptive about the blood.

This was an impulsive night, so I snatched a pen that still lay on the table where I kept the book before Endymion stole it. Underneath his writing, I responded, *Because darkness makes light seem brighter.*

I read on.

Panicked for her shepherd, Genevieve called for aid but no one dwelled in the depth of the forest. She was alone with the wolf, whom he had stabbed in the eye and mouth so deeply that its face seemed a mass of bloody tissue, and her dying beloved, who would never know her true identity or her true feelings for him.

Among the trees, a mossy rock moved. Genevieve's confusion and terror grew. Was this another enemy? The rock shuffled forward... and raised its head. A woman with the features of an old woman but the smooth skin of a young one peered out from beneath a mounded cloak loaded with forest debris.

Beside this paragraph, Endymion had written, *G cannot distinguish witch from rock?*

To which I responded, *She's traumatized.*

I continued. In the story, the witch grants Genevieve a magical healing potion in exchange for an answer to a question.

The princess agrees and revives Orlando. The witch asks who killed the wolf—I had planned to have her return for revenge since the wolf had been her beloved pet, but never got around to writing that episode—and then disappears, leaving the couple alone. Once more becoming too descriptive, I spent two whole pages of tiny writing explaining their kisses and desire. My face burned to read it again.

It didn't help that this section in particular now had many comments and questions written in.

Is the eviscerated wolf still lying there?

Why will she not reveal the truth to him now that he has proved his love to her?

And, most of all, one tiny note scratched in the corner made my heart drop.

Is this what you like?

I pinched the pen in my fingers, but couldn't bring myself to respond. I set about addressing the rest of Endymion's questions wherever there was room. (I had forgotten all about the bloody wolf in the throes of imagining the love scene.)

The next chapter contained an even shorter story about the lovers running from royal guards. Apparently, they were always running from something. I answered all of the questions in the margins there too before returning to that little one a few pages back.

At first, his vandalism of my book had clearly been about mining it for information. That was before he realized it was fiction. None of the books in the small library were fictional, so perhaps he expected everything he read to contain facts or theories pertaining to the real world with no embellishments. What a dry existence! These notes, by contrast, focused more on the characters and his interest in understanding their motivations. Of course, he also pointed out absurdities where he found them with an eye as keen as a tactician's.

By the end, some of the notes he wrote weren't just about the story, but about me.

Is this what you like?

Up ahead, toward the final pages of the book, was one more love scene before their doomed ending. It hadn't been marked before, but I turned there now, pulse beating in my throat.

One section had been newly underlined.

That's twice. I have my answer.

My pen hovered over the words. I couldn't deny it, but it felt indecent to confirm it as well. If I let him read this book again, he would notice the comments to which I hadn't replied. I *would* let him borrow the book again, I realized. His last attempt to rid himself of the shadows hadn't worked, so he would undoubtedly leave on another trip soon. If he wanted to take *Tales of Orlando and Genevieve*, he could. I'd leave it in the library for him. My skin tingled with the idea that he might read those illicit passages again, as I had.

As I closed the cover, a smudge on one of the blank end pages caught my eye.

Is there more?

I smiled, closed the book, and tried to sleep.

19

When I squinted open my eyes the next morning, somebody stood in my room. I jolted upright, hair flying.

It was Ellis.

She stood as calmly as ever, but her expression held a new scrutiny. Did she know about Endymion's confessions of last night?

Pursing her lips, she examined me from my unbraided hair to the lumps of my knees under the covers.

"You and my son seem distracted," she said without preamble, "chasing your little deception. I, however, have remained focused. You never told us the origin of the golden brush or the markings on your skin. They might contain the clue we need to defeat the Enemy and now..." She let the word drift off in disgust, as though I'd done wrong or lured the King toward frivolity with his realm on the line.

I glanced at the markings to make sure they were still there.

"He cannot afford to lose focus, especially not for some girl he found wandering in the woods. We have taken you in, given you shelter, and fed you our delicacies, but I will not allow this ruse to become anything more than the barest stratagem toward victory."

I'd never heard Ellis speak so much. It was impossible to contradict someone so authoritarian. I saw where Endymion got the commanding part of his personality. Also, I still lay in bed, which seemed a lazy position to be caught in. No matter that it was still undoubtedly morning.

"From today, you will have no contact with the King apart from mandated events that require your attendance. The rest of your time will be spent here, in the lower level. There is no longer any need for you to loiter aboveground. If you must fetch something, either I or Calyse will accompany you."

I could hardly process all the information hurling at me with the speed of an angry swarm of bees. "What did I do wrong?" I stammered.

"I encountered the King last night as he was returning to his room and he divulged that you had cornered him in the library."

"*I* had cornered *him*?" I exclaimed, incredulous. "I merely couldn't sleep. I didn't expect to find him there—"

"Your excuses mean little to someone who has heard them all. He can afford no distractions."

"What... did he say?"

"You declared your love for him. It's no wonder—"

My snort cut her off. I had done no such thing. Was that how he had interpreted my kiss? It was ludicrous. It seemed odd too that he would tell his mother immediately after I left. I didn't know Endymion very well, but I doubted he gushed to his mother about the passion he experienced with Rose. So why lie to her?

Suddenly, the truth became clear. My love was a safer lie than the damning reality that he had confided everything to me about the shadows, about Im Scathail's possession, about all the things that could dismantle the Other Kingdom.

This verbal persecution was minor compared to the assassination that could have ensued if anyone knew what had really passed between us in the library.

"I'm sorry," I said. "You caught me by surprise. I'm already engaged to the King; I didn't think it would be wrong to love him as well."

"Love is a luxury. But you are a mortal girl, unused to higher duty," Ellis replied. "Save your passion for a consort."

Gratefulness filled me that I finally knew enough to interpret her words. Ellis and Calyse held the apocalyptic secret that, through dark magic forged by his love's death, their King was also the Shadow. Endymion could not love because it would end in destruction, not because he lacked the capacity.

I dropped my head submissively, hoping that would be enough to prompt the older woman to leave.

Evidently, it was, because Ellis only stayed to reiterate her basic instructions before blowing out of the room like a storm cloud.

No unnecessary contact with the King.

No unchaperoned visits aboveground.

Ellis' outburst fueled my budding rebelliousness. I dragged the large book from the side table and set it on my crossed legs. Turning to the end pages, I wrote, *Yes, there will be more, but you must wait for it.*

Once I was certain I wouldn't encounter Ellis in the hallway, I emerged, dressed in a thin blue gown. On my way to the dining room, I dropped off my book in the library, where I was sure Endymion would find it. To my own surprise, I tingled with anticipation to see what he would write next.

Shaking off the feeling, I sought out food. I realized just

before I stepped through the door that I was humming the song I'd learned in childhood:

"We must not look at goblin men,

We must not buy their fruits:

Who knows upon what soil they fed

Their hungry thirsty roots?"

All goblin men were dangerous—the term applied to forest creatures and Fae alike, anyone inhuman. My own mother, in Ellis' place, might set the same ultimatums if she feared for her child. I thawed a little toward the old woman, but I didn't intend to fully obey.

Calyse sat at the far end of the table, not the seat he ordinarily chose, looking deeply pensive. His head rested on clasped hands and his eyes were far away.

When he noticed me, he beamed, dispelling the gloom from a moment before. "Laura!" he greeted. "I'm sorry I have not been able to offer you my congratulations." He rose from the table and took my pale hand in his, raising it to his lips.

Had the King not told his best friend that the betrothal was a farce? I decided to play along. "Thank you. I know the King appreciates all you do for him, and so do I."

He smiled warmly, indicating for me to take a seat beside him. "End can be a stubborn bastard, so I'm glad someone other than me sees his better side. He really is the best of us, when he's not the worst." He laughed.

I had started to come to that conclusion myself. Endymion was still an enigma, but the unfolding layers revealed someone sad and perhaps even good.

I shook myself, heaping my plate with roasted squash and sweet bread. After a few bites, I regarded Calyse. "You know I've seen the... shadows. Is there any way I can help him be free of those?"

"No. It's what I think about all the time. We've explored a thousand paths and found no cure. I had to take up flute playing to get my mind off it." He gave a low chuckle. "Actually, I always liked playing. It drives End crazy, which is only another reason to love it." He squared his massive shoulders. "If there were some way for you to help, one of us would have told you already."

I would find out for myself. Especially if Ellis was going to try to keep me away from her son, I would research how to free him and how to free my sister, whose time was running out. End would hear about any solution I discovered.

Calyse stuffed an entire roll in his mouth. I watched him anxiously, hoping he wouldn't choke. Could that happen to semi-immortal beings?

"I'm glad," he managed as he swallowed, "that I'll get to see your confirmation ceremony at least."

I perked up. "My what?"

Calyse pivoted his body toward me in pleased astonishment. "You mean he didn't tell you when you had your tryst last night? He is baffling..." With a deep breath, he explained, "The confirmation ceremony sanctions your engagement. It makes it official."

"What is it like?" Just when I thought I understood this world, I plunged right back into childish ignorance. I had thought the party had been all the confirmation our betrothal needed.

"You both strip naked before a large crowd and you carve your initial into each other's chests before you..."

The blood drained entirely from my face. Freezing sweat coated my neck.

Calyse's serious expression broke and he guffawed with laughter. Wiping a tear delicately from his eye, he said, "Oh, your face! No, no. You just stand before the Oakmaiden. A few family and friends are there. She approves the potential union. That's it. No public sexuality required." He collected himself, finally, as my cold sweat gave way to a burning blush. "It's later today, so I'm glad you encountered someone who could inform you about it."

After the confirmation ceremony, Calyse would prepare for yet another of Endymion's journeys, he said, and I would go to find answers.

20

Endymion and I walked arm in arm through the enormous arcade toward the Rose Room. Unsaid things crackled in the air between us, but we didn't speak. Ellis, Calyse, and a few others walked behind. I felt his mood, which had become apprehensive. Despite our nearness, his profile revealed little attention on me.

I tried not to be disappointed.

The guards parted to allow us entrance. Roses floated in thin troughs of water, the metalwork on the door and walls exquisite. My heart twisted for Endymion, and I wondered how often he came here, if at all. Once in the Oakmaiden's presence, shadowed by her permanently autumnal leaves, the audience took their places in the tiered wooden seats. The King and I faced the seer. Her expression was solemn, as before, her body stretched and beautiful, even covered in the skin of the tree. She appeared to look at us. Evidently, Endymion was more worthy of notice than a mortal girl.

"Great Oakmaiden, we are here for the confirmation ceremony," the King announced in his deep voice. He wasn't one for preamble.

"King," whispered the Oakmaiden like rushing wind, "who do you intend to wed?" Her eyes grew deeper, becoming black pits.

"This mortal woman, Laura of Selene." He nodded toward me.

Only now did I consider there could be consequences to breaking this betrothal. Endymion did not intend to marry me, only to prolong the engagement. As the temperature in the room dropped, my hairs stood on end. This ceremony felt perilously close to a vow. My new sense of rebellion hadn't shaken my desire to live by my word. Perhaps that was silly now that I lived a lie.

Wind blew around us, whipping the King's hair around his golden ear ornaments and flapping my skirt against my legs.

The blackness of the Oakmaiden's eyes grew, spidering out in lines across her face as though she were a burnt statue. "A prophecy pertains to your marriage," she said, pitching higher like screeching wind.

Endymion did not move, though I had to fight not to sway with the tempest swirling around us. I was glad to have braided my hair today so I could see, even if hearing and standing were becoming difficult. The King tightened his hold on my arm.

The Oakmaiden repeated the prophecy about his marriage to a mortal ending the war, and then the wind died enough for me to focus. Disheveled and breathless, I cast a glance at Endymion, whose jaw was set. Happily, his back faced the crowd, so they couldn't see how serious he was. I assume that most confirmations were joyous occasions, although the sight of the Oakmaiden channeling prophecies chilled my blood.

"Is this a marriage of duty or love?" asked the ancient seer.

The question surprised me. Why did it matter?

Duty was the answer, but he said, "Love."

This must be part of the curse, I thought. *Only love would bind us together strongly enough for the prophecy to work.*

The Oakmaiden appeared to lift her brown chin slightly, though I couldn't be sure. "Present the offerings."

From behind us, Calyse, Ellis, and the others processed around the far side that I hadn't explored the first time I'd come here. They emerged with copper cups in their hands, half-filled with liquid. What kind, I wasn't sure. One by one, they marched in the space between us and the roots of the Oakmaiden and poured their offerings into the round hole in the floor. Calyse winked at me, no doubt remembering his joke from earlier about how the ceremony entailed standing naked with Endymion before a swarm of spectators. I huffed good-naturedly at him.

When the guests had returned to their seats, the Oakmaiden spoke again. "Life spilled here confirms your impending union. King Endymion and Laura of Selene, your engagement is established."

With a wooden creak, she lowered one of her upraised arms, its yellow leaves trembling. Releasing me, Endymion stepped forward. He touched the thin end of the branch almost like a caress, letting his fingers trail before gently breaking off a single leaf. He held it reverently between his thumb and forefinger and stepped back.

As the Oakmaiden lifted the branch once again, I noticed scarring along one side. Shards were missing, peeled away from her skin. On such an otherwise gorgeous tree, the small mutilation stood out in relief. Perhaps that was what Endymion had been so careful to touch.

Applause broke out behind us. We turned and the King raised the leaf high.

Calyse grinned and Ellis looked placid. Her words from that

morning crept under my skin. I was not to see the King except for official reasons like this one. I took his arm once more.

"Give her a kiss," Calyse suggested.

The bottom of my stomach dropped. I didn't look at Endymion, assuming he would take that as encouragement.

Ellis scowled at the dark Fae.

Despite her displeasure, a celebratory atmosphere a little reminiscent of the betrothal party permeated the atmosphere. Yes, this event was serious but the hope that Endymion's marriage gave to his kingdom welled up in bubbling exhilaration.

Calyse was one of the only Fae who knew about the King's shadows, but perhaps End hadn't told him everything, how the prophecy had led to the destruction he was working to undo.

"Go on," Calyse insisted.

I felt their eyes on me. If we were truly marrying for love, as the King claimed, we wouldn't look so somber at our own confirmation ceremony. But my heart had started beating wildly, and I didn't know what to do.

Endymion tugged his arm free, pivoting me toward him. I searched his golden eyes, trying to discover what he was thinking. Did he really intend to kiss me, here, in front of everyone? Had I led him to believe I wanted that because of my behavior at the party and the kiss on the cheek last night?

His lips twitched up in the smallest of smiles, the first I had seen that day. Finally, I could read something in his expression.

He would, if I would.

I could no longer breathe. My head bobbed with such a tiny movement that it could have been a mere tremor, but he saw it for what it was. Permission.

He hooked one long finger under my chin, lingering there. His preternaturally beautiful face drew close to mine, his warm breath teasing my mouth. Then he surged forward the remaining distance, his soft lips covering mine. His spice-and-moss scent invaded my senses and I closed my eyes. I leaned in against him, pressing my mouth to his, a wild craving swelling up inside me for more. I felt drunk again, desperate. Goosebumps sprang up along my neck and arms. His touch was tender, yet deeply, wickedly sensual.

When he broke the kiss, I blinked. It had happened in the span of three seconds. I heard Calyse laughing happily. Movement. People leaving.

I looked tentatively at Endymion. Had he felt heat and longing flood his body too? The intensity of my reaction unsettled me. The kiss had been chaste, yet my mind instantly conjured images that were definitely not.

He returned my look, but I could read nothing of his emotions.

I tried to catch my breath. *This is a false engagement. There is more at stake than your lustful emotions, Laura.*

But no matter what I told myself, I knew I would welcome another kiss.

21

"Why are you avoiding me?" Endymion leaned back in his chair like a cat at ease. He was leaving today, and looked ready in his dark leathers. He fixed me with a curious look.

"I'm not avoiding you," I replied. He had just returned from a very short trip taken after the confirmation ceremony. It was true that we hadn't seen each other for several days. I didn't know what to think after our kiss. Ellis had forbidden me to talk to Endymion outside of mandated events, and my own feelings tangled so tightly that I threw myself into reading instead. Every night the memory returned of his warm lips pressed against mine.

Calyse had just left, having finished his breakfast, and we were alone in the dining room.

"Did I upset you?"

"No."

"Did I overstep?"

"No."

"Are you afraid of me?"

I paused. Strange as it was, even after the shadows attacked me, I didn't fear him. "No."

He took a swig of juice. "Then you're certainly acting strangely."

"I thought I wasn't supposed to talk to you."

He tipped forward. "Who told you that?"

"Your mother."

He scoffed. "She would say something like that. I am the King. She is not. You may talk to me if you wish."

"I don't want to anger her."

"Don't worry about her. I'll talk to her."

"And tell her that I..." *Love you?* But the question didn't materialize. It felt too close to the feeling churning inside me now. I didn't want to aggravate it from feral attraction into actual liking or love.

I felt on edge, unsure, eager to go but desperate to stay. I hardly knew myself anymore.

End finished his juice and set down the glass. "That you what?"

"She doesn't know that I know, does she? Calyse doesn't either." I couldn't say the truth aloud, even here, in case someone overheard.

The King hummed, a deep, throaty sound like a growl. I knew he was the Shadow, that Im Scathail had possessed him. That knowledge could break the kingdom. "No, I didn't tell them."

"So you lied instead."

"Is it so farfetched that you would be smitten with me?" His indecent smirk sent a shiver down my limbs.

He stood, suddenly weighed down again by burdens by trying to stay cheerful for me. I saw it all in the lines of his muscular shoulders. "Maybe this will be the one," he said. The trip that would free him of the Shadow. But his golden eyes hollowed with despair.

"Maybe it will," I said seriously.

"Let's hope so, for everyone's sake." He paused at the door. "By the way, the reading material on my journeys has become much more interesting over time. I recommend it." Humor danced over his features, his amber eyes glittering, and then he left.

I barely waited a heartbeat after his quiet footsteps faded to sweep toward the little library. There, on the shelf where I'd left it, was my book. I grabbed it and practically ran back to my room. Today, I had nothing to do but more research, and Calyse had promised to send forest creatures to fetch herbs for me to use in experimental potions.

That meant I could use the late morning to read what End had written in my book. Only the Fae attendants would interrupt with their daily bath. Calyse had promised to return at night.

I flipped to the final page first.

Is there more? he had written.

Yes, there will be more, but you must wait for it.

An answer, in the smallest writing so far, as though he wanted to save most of the page for me, read, *I've waited my entire life. It must be now.*

I swallowed. This flirtation eased the stressfulness of both our lives without sending us into the danger that Ellis described. These little notes were like little caresses, and I hoped there were more.

Tentatively, I returned to the question I hadn't addressed.

Is this what you like? Beside it, he had written. *You didn't answer the question, little thorn. Am I to interpret this silence however I want?*

My pulse thundered in my ears. I held the pen, but still wavered above the page.

Flirtation—nothing more.

You can imagine it however you want as well.

Exhaling sharply, I threw the pen to the side as though I hadn't guided it through every letter. The naughty implication would make Endymion smile. I told myself it was to ease his monumental troubles. I knew, though, that I'd meant every word.

I returned to safer ground.

What happened to O's flock after they ran away together? he asked. So he had found more plot holes.

I groaned. Never did I expect the King of the Fae to scrutinize my every word.

I spent the morning in bed, pouring over his comments, replying where there was room and devising what I might write next in the additional pages. No story came to me. My own tale filled my mind.

Eventually, I set the book aside and worked on adjusting known charms. I knew I probably couldn't cure Endymion with a human remedy, but perhaps I could reduce the effects of the curse. My mind returned to Lizzie, asleep on that cot. If only there was something I could do for her. But I could help no one, only distract or delay.

My excitement of the morning faded into afternoon malaise. I combined jasmine and St. John's wort. I even added a drop of my own blood pricked from a finger. The swirling liquid in the little bottle glittered in the pale light of the fire, but I had no one to test its contents on but myself, and I wasn't ill. In fact, during my time in Tylaith Castle, I'd grown even healthier than before. I never suffered hunger pains, my skin looked shining and smooth, and my mind felt more capable, even though the riddles it attempted to solve were greater here than any from back home. I had lost a little muscle from not working in the garden. I missed that. It was kind of Calyse and the attendants to bring me the herbs I requested, but I would have preferred to grow them myself.

I set the mixture aside. It combined two remedies I felt confident would work well together—one for dulling pain and another for expelling disease. I left out ingredients that would lend themselves to sleep.

May you sleep short and live long.

The door opened and Calyse stepped inside. Fae, with their preternatural quietness, never seemed to care about privacy unless I was invading theirs.

I was glad to see him, though.

"Laura," he said with a preoccupied smile. He wore dark leathers as though he were about to leave the castle on one of Endymion's trips.

"Is everything all right?" I asked.

"I'm here to tell you that instead of leaving again, End is staying here tonight. We think the remedy might work just as well inside the castle. There's no additional piece to track down." I saw his broad chest rise and fall with nervous relief.

My brows furrowed. "Why are you telling me this?" They usually kept such secrecy around End's missions and the objects he found to expel the evil from his body.

"You might hear some... noises tonight."

"Noises? Like what?"

"Just don't be alarmed. I'm doing everything I can for him. A few others will be there too. There is a small group of us—you know—who are dedicated to helping him."

"There's nothing I can do to help?" My gut roiled at the thought of what kinds of noises I'd have to endure without being able to do something.

Calyse smiled sadly, then brightened. "No, the pain is simply something he has to endure. Thoughts of you might aid him."

"Won't... won't the whole castle hear if he..." I couldn't say the rest.

If he's screaming.

"The lower level is well insulated. We made the changes after the Great Sleep when we discovered what had happened. End needed a place he could go that was forbidden to everyone else."

"Except for you," I said, trying for lightness.

"And you." He winked. "So, don't fear. It will be over soon."

I felt my heart in my throat. Nodding, I handed Calyse the new potion I'd just made. "Can you give him this? It might not do anything, but..."

He pressed it back in my hands. "I can't take the chance that that will react with what we're using already," he said.

I gripped the neck of the bottle, another wave of uselessness washing over me.

"Take care of him," I said quietly.

"I'll do my best. I promise."

⚜

IT MUST HAVE BEEN WELL PAST MIDNIGHT WHEN I FELL ASLEEP, exhausted from listening for the promised sounds of Endymion in distress. No noises punctuated the crackling silence. I drifted uneasily, reality blurring with dreams. At one point I thought I had risen and searched for him down the hallway which had become tortuously twisted, leading to blind corners and endless passages. I found only sightless maidens and drops of blood leading under locked doors.

I jolted from sleep when a strangled cry cut off suddenly. Had I really heard it? I sat up, pulse racing, and looked toward the darkened door. Only the faint firelight illuminated the room, the flames burned down to embers. Perhaps I hadn't heard anything at all... Calyse had said not to be alarmed, though.

In spite of his warnings, alarm coursed through my veins into my very extremities. Sleep was impossible now. I dwelt in a twilight state. As soon as I would begin to drift off, I'd jerk back to attention, seeking out those cries of Endymion in pain. No other shouts or moans sliced through the air. Was I simply too far away to hear? Had their painful remedy actually worked?

Remembering Endymion's face from this morning, I too doubted that this method—whatever it was—would cure him. How, then, would he rid himself of the shadows?

I ached for him, bearing a secret so terrible that it could cost him his throne, if not the lives of everyone in the kingdom.

A knock on the door.

I leapt up. No one knocked. Everyone just entered at their will. I, a mortal girl, was not given the luxury of a private space.

Padding barefoot to the door through the darkness, I opened it a crack. At eye level was a muscular chest in a torn shirt with shadows curling off it like smoke. I raised my eyes. Endymion, golden eyes red-rimmed, looked down at me, breathless. I couldn't tell if he was still in pain from whatever potion or procedure he'd endured, or if he had run. No matter the case, he looked as vulnerable as I'd seen him since the day he collapsed on my threshold.

"Your book... wasn't in the library." On an exhale, his face crumpled.

Was the King of the Fae about to cry in my doorway?

I opened the door wider to let him in and quickly lit two candles to give a little more light. The darkness around Endymion made him hard to see in the dimness, but the shadows didn't multiply as they had that one day. It didn't seem as if they would attack.

"I forgot to put it back," I muttered, placing an arm around his back and leading him further into the room to show I wasn't frightened.

We sat on the edge of the bed. He took my hands in his rough ones and shut his eyes tight. He raised our joined hands and leaned his forehead against them. For a while, he merely breathed. I searched for signs of injury but found none apart from the torn clothes and smudges that appeared to be dirt on his skin and hair. The shadows wreathed around my fingers, feeling them, caressing them.

Finally, his voice came out deep and broken. "Tell me a different ending."

22

My heart broke, but I wasn't sure what he meant. Did he want a new fictional story about true love conquering death instead of succumbing to it? Did he want me to find a real solution for him?

"I've made a new healing charm," I said, suddenly remembering. "It could help with the pain." I released him and fetched the little bottle from the hearth. "I don't know how well it will work, but the ingredients are innocuous on their own, so even if they don't dull all the pain, they can't hurt you." I knocked the bottle against my fingertip.

I realized too late that there was no need for me to administer the potion. He could take the healing charm himself. I scraped the drop off my finger.

"I..." He looked exhausted enough to collapse.

"Come on," I said, acting for all the world like my mother. "Let's get you cleaned up and then you can sleep."

I hardly remembered Endymion ever looking so slovenly. Even when I first interrupted him in the library, he'd been tousled but never dirty. I doubted he liked to appear less than pristine.

I managed to keep conscious thoughts away as I ushered Endymion to the circular pool. The churning water looked black. I realized that the three Fae attendants who always cleaned me never left their soap or sponges here.

"You can wash off," I said, less certainly, peering down. "If you want to."

Without further prompting, he removed his torn shirt. I stood speechless at the sight of the ridged expanse of his well-muscled chest. Shadows and dirt obscured it, but his beauty surpassed any man I'd ever encountered. His hips swelled above low-slung trousers, drawing my eyes downward.

He tossed the shirt to the side carelessly and began to remove the rest of his clothing.

Utterly overwhelmed, I averted my eyes, seeing his gorgeous form no matter where I looked. The water lapped and I trusted he was in the pool. Beside the bath were piled his shirt and trousers, both dirtied. Only Endymion's powerful arms sprawled luxuriously along the edge of the pool and half his torso showed above the water. Everything else was too dark. I released a breath.

He closed his eyes once again, but whether in mental or physical pain, I wasn't sure.

I stood awkwardly at the edge of the pool in my nightgown. "Would you like that potion?" I asked, voice small. The events unfolding around me seemed too big for me to do anything of consequence. How could I help someone as great as Endymion?

"Yes."

I turned to collect it.

"But more than that," he said, "I want a new ending."

"Excuse me?"

He opened his eyes, frustrated. "That story. Orlando and Genevieve. I need to know... I don't like the ending."

He didn't only mean Orlando and Genevieve.

I brought the bottle to him. "Here you are."

He didn't touch it. "Please, Laura." He rarely used my name. I softened at the sound of it. At home, I heard it all the time. Not here.

I rifled through ideas for stories that I'd been considering for the final pages. Nothing fit. "You want me to rewrite the ending?"

He looked at me then with such honest fear and exhaustion and pain in his eyes that my heart skipped. "I need to know it can be different," he whispered.

Embers glowed in the hearth. Morning hadn't come. No doubt Endymion had crept out of bed. I doubted Calyse would have left him alone like this. Everything felt unreal and also as authentic as thoughts hidden from the world.

I touched the water with my toe. Warm, as always. By now I was used to stripping for my daily bath. Neoma and the other attendants saw me all the time. I wavered, breath shallow.

"Once upon a time," I began, raising my nightgown over my head, "there lived a shepherd named Orlando. The shepherd worked in the fields within sight of the castle called Roset. Within Roset dwelled a maiden named Genevieve. She fell deeply in love with Orlando. One day, after seeing him defeat an enormous wolf attacking his flock, she invited him to the palace."

I set my nightgown on top of Endymion's clothes. He was so glorious that I felt freckled and skinny and unworthy by comparison, but I slipped into the opposite side of the bath nonetheless.

He watched me with glowing eyes. His pained expression began to clear.

"When the King discovered that Genevieve had invited a lowly shepherd to the palace, he intercepted him and said he must complete three challenges to earn his daughter's love."

The water lapped over my breasts, but in this non-time, I felt beyond consequence. Dirt still smeared End's face. I swished forward as I continued.

"The first task was to kill a monstrous snake that consumed travelers on the way to his kingdom."

I raised my hand out of the water and rubbed my callused thumb against his gritty cheek, washing the dirt away. He watched me closely.

"The second was to find the golden egg of a mythical bird on the edge of the highest cliff."

He raised his hand now and trailed wet fingers along the line of my jaw.

"The third was to move a huge statue of the King from one end of the kingdom to the other."

I finished cleaning his face and scooped some water up for his hair. Rivulets ran down his face like tears. I rubbed his scalp, threading my fingers through his hair once, twice.

His groaned and his hands found the bare skin of my sides and pulled me to him. The tips of my breasts brushed his strong chest and his full mouth dipped close to mine. Frozen there, we let the water lap around us, almost uncomfortably hot between the heated water and our heated skin.

Finally, I twisted so I could rest my back against his chest. He held me as he had on the throne during the party, with his hand splayed across my middle, running his thumb lazily across my navel. Against my lower back, I felt his erection. It was almost inconceivable that I, a no-name country girl from a mortal town, could find myself in the arms of the Fae King.

I reveled in the sensation, but I wasn't ready yet to act on those feelings. Endymion was vulnerable. He needed comfort and sleep.

"Orlando went to find the snake," I continued in a husky voice. "'Why do you kill?' he said. The snake replied, 'So everyone will know my name.' 'I know of something that no being can accomplish.' The snake bared its fangs. 'I could do it,' the snake boasted."

"Move the statue." End's hot breath stirred my hair as he murmured his guess.

"Yes. The snake was so large that it could pick up the statue and move it from one end of the kingdom to the other. It struggled to accomplish the task as Orlando watched. Finally, Orlando praised the snake, saying, 'You did what no other being could do.' As the snake creature preened with pride, Orlando struck it unaware."

"Poor snake," End muttered, stroking my hair.

"There was only one task left—to retrieve the egg from the highest cliff. To accomplish this, Orlando resolved to climb. He was strong from his time as a shepherd, and his love for Genevieve kept him reaching, hand over hand, even after the drop became terrifying and his hands became bloody. When he finally reached the top, he discovered he had climbed the wrong cliff. The King had provided him with wrong directions so he could push him to his doom and prevent him from ever marrying his daughter."

The hand against my stomach tightened. "This is a new ending?"

"Yes." I twisted to look at Endymion, who frowned, wet hair clinging to his face. Untidy and concerned, he had never looked so handsome. My blood beat heavily in my neck and low in my core. "Genevieve heard about the deception and rode to rescue her love Orlando. Afraid she was too late, she spurred her horse faster. Finally, upon reaching the cliff, she saw no sign of Orlando."

"Where is he?" End asked gruffly.

"He had figured out the plot against him and had hidden within sight of the cliff's edge to watch for anyone who wanted to push him off. Distraught, Genevieve called his name, convinced that he was dead."

"Why do you put them through all this?" His mouth was against my hair now. I fought to keep my breathing even with little success.

"'Orlando!'" she called. "She fell to the ground in grief. Just then, Orlando appeared from his hiding place."

"He took long enough to appear."

"And he lifted Genevieve from her knees and kissed her. She promised right then to help him with his final task."

"Finding the egg."

I nodded. "They looked at maps to determine which cliff in the kingdom truly was the tallest. One had no path from the top, but could only be gained by climbing straight up. The egg was surely there."

Endymion's thumb hadn't stopped moving, lulling me almost into a trance.

"On the morning of the climb, Genevieve discovered that her father had posted archers around the cliff with orders to strike any climbers. None of the archers would ever strike a princess, she realized, so she had to make the climb herself. Orlando begged her not to go, but she knew it was the only way."

"She shouldn't put herself in danger. What if they don't recognize her?"

"And Orlando should? They're in danger either way."

"Should I trust you, little thorn?"

Desire spiked in my stomach, but I simply said, "As a storyteller, yes. Let me tell it."

He adjusted me against himself. I felt every muscle of his against my back.

Short of breath, I continued, "On the appointed day, Genevieve started the climb. She reached up one hand, then the other. The top of the cliff was so high it was lost in the clouds. Determined to complete the tasks for her love, she struggled onward. But when she reached the middle of the cliff, one of the archers loosed an arrow and struck her."

"What?" End snapped. "She dies?"

"She's not dead. Orlando finds her crumpled body at the foot of the cliff and performs magic to make her live."

"Sounds like the witch," he huffed.

I smiled. "The King was so touched by the force of their love and by how much they were willing to sacrifice for each other that he changed his earlier edict and allowed them to marry. Orlando moved into the castle and they were wed and lived happily ever after." I twisted to see the King's profile in the dying light. "Is that a better ending?"

"Happily..." he murmured. "I like that."

Silence fell thick and anticipatory around us.

"I like that too," I whispered, too aware of each place where his skin touched mine.

He moved first, spinning me around once again to face him. Even the sluggish resistance of the water reinforced the dreamlike quality of what was happening. His gaze burned like fire, though the gold had become a hair-thin ring around his dilated pupils. His sensual mouth and strong arms beckoned me forward. He held me to him, pressing skin to skin. Need throbbed between my legs, aching, insisting.

Slowly, his mouth met mine, soft and full. I moaned as he deepened the kiss. This was so much more than the slight press at the confirmation ceremony. Now he held me tight around my waist and upper back, opening his mouth to invite me to taste him. I licked his tongue and the rim of his lips, warm spices lingering there. Our mouths moved together, exploratory and yearning. My sensitive breasts against his muscles heightened my sensation.

He walked us backward, still holding me, until my back pressed against the rim of the pool. His body followed, pushing me back until I felt all of him—his chest, his arms, his legs, his erection at my stomach, his mouth on mine. Shadows wreathed around us both, and the reminder just made me more frantic, more desperate.

I cried out as he rolled his hips against me, teasing the sensitive part at my center. He took advantage of how I'd broken the kiss to draw his teeth lightly against my exposed neck. He thrust again as he licked. I gave into sensation, helpless in his strong arms.

He nipped and licked my neck, then my lips, sucking them as if they held the very remedy he needed.

My own whimpering noises brought me suddenly back to the present, where I arched against Endymion, exposing myself to him like a delicacy to be tasted and torn apart. I slowed my breathing. My trembling hand found his hair, and I pulled his head from between my breasts.

Panting, I attempted to ease myself out of the bath. "We should get some sleep."

Taking his cue, Endymion backed away, dripping. His chest rose and fell compulsively too. We looked like long-distance swimmers.

"You need rest," I repeated. "You've been through a lot tonight. I shouldn't have kept you up."

He ran both hands back through his hair to restore it to some kind of order. "On the contrary, I needed a new ending. And I believed for a moment there could be one. You've helped me tremendously." He eased himself up out of the pool. I took in his strong thighs, the swell of his ass, the V down to his...

I turned away again. Who was I? What was this? The haze of desire made it hard to think properly. I didn't like the thought of getting my only nightgown wet so I rushed to get under the covers as I was. My sopping hair soaked into the main pillow I used, though there were several on the large bed.

I watched End through slitted eyes for a moment.

"You can stay if you want to." The words came from me. I could hardly have been more surprised if someone else had entered the room and declared them.

He accepted my offer without a word, doing as I had and leaving his dry clothes on the edge of the pool. Crawling into bed, he turned in the opposite direction, leaving me my side of the mattress.

I scooted closer and cast an arm around him, holding him as we both fell asleep.

❧ 23 ❧

When I woke, Endymion was gone. The little bottle of potion still sat on the rim of the bath on a sliver of white marble. My black nightgown pooled beside it. Those were the only two pieces of evidence that last night had actually happened.

I hugged the silk coverlet closer to my chin. What boldness had possessed me to bathe with the King, tell him stories, kiss him with such hungry need? I couldn't shake the aftereffect of longing. His absence in the morning didn't surprise me. The Fae with their ability to appear and disappear so quietly it seemed like magic made it inevitable. But it disappointed me nonetheless. I'd hoped to feel his strong back warm against my front when I awoke.

Ellis' words returned to me. *He can afford no distractions.*

And Endymion's explanation of love among the Fae: *Love, when we encounter it, is all-consuming. It's an obsession, a flame that won't burn out.*

That couldn't be what had begun to spark between us. Endymion demonstrated no obsession, only a curiosity about me

—perhaps a lustful one, it was true, but with no all-consuming love attached. Ellis was right. More than anything, I was a distraction.

Rallying, I rose and replaced the healing charm on the dying hearth. Choosing the deep blue gown, I changed and went straight to the library, bringing with me the book of stories. If I had time, I would write down the ending I had told Endymion. In the meantime, I would leave it on the shelf for him to read any time he wished.

Fiction had sustained me through times of fear or boredom so many times throughout my life that it was difficult to conceive how unacquainted he was with anything but books of war or magical objects.

This time I chose the books written in the Fae language, trying to match the letters to the prophecy written on my shoulder. An idea had come to me in my sleep. What if there were more prophecies about Im Scathail that could shed light on a solution? Or, in the absence of that, was there a chance that the Oakmaiden herself could proclaim a new prophecy amending the old one? Did she receive her words from some mysterious, supernatural source, or did she bring the truth of them into being?

"Ah, there you are," said Cal, entering the dim room where I sat at the table like an obsessed mage, peering at no less than four open books. "You missed breakfast this morning. I think that must be the first time."

"I slept in," I muttered, hoping he wouldn't notice my blush.

"I'm glad you could sleep through our applying the rune stones. I keep telling End that those won't work. We've seen it time and time again, but he won't listen to me. He gets hurt every time."

"How is End this morning?"

I realized my error too late. When had I started thinking of the King by his nickname? Had I said it aloud before? I glanced at Cal, whose lips twisted knowingly.

"He's... better than last night."

"Good." I returned to the manuscripts.

"What are you looking for in here? Do you speak Fae?"

"No," I admitted, turning the page of one book that looked promising. I had already distinguished a few words from my golden tattoo written there, though not in the right order. "I'm looking for more prophecies regarding the war. I understand the one on my arm, but surely there must be more. This conflict has persisted for hundreds of years."

"There are more. You need only have asked. Your obsession with study makes me think you're trying to solve this on your own. You know that's foolish." He raised an eyebrow, though his tone was not unkind. Unspoken were the words, *And you're merely a human.*

"Can you help me, then?" I wasn't going to sit in my room all day getting dressed up like a princess without doing something to help. If Im Scathail wasn't stopped, according to everything I'd read, his darkness would infect not only Endymion, not only the Fae kingdom, but the mortal one as well. Selene lay just at the border of the barrier. It would be among the first to fall. Simple fairy fruit caused maidens to waste away in helpless longing until they died before their time, mere husks of who they had been. The face of the withered dead girl burned my memory. Even enchanted sleep wasn't enough to preserve her forever.

"I can't help for long. *End*"—he emphasized the name a bit more strenuously than usual—"is in an absolute frenzy to find a solution. He's already announced a new location, a new attempt, and I'm going with him." Cal stood tall, warriorlike in his leather armor. "A few others need to go as well. This one is heavily guarded, which gives him hope this might be enough to reverse the effects of..." He wobbled his head for me to finished the thought.

"When are you leaving?" The idea of Endymion and Cal leaving for what sounded like more than only a day or two left me more bereft than I would have thought.

Cal's voice softened, lines of concern crossing his dark features. "He's still weak from yesterday, so we'll wait a couple days, but he insists we must leave after that."

I didn't like Cal's obvious worry. I swallowed. "Can you tell me the rest of the prophecies today?"

"I don't have time, unfortunately. Lots of preparation to do." He wandered to the shelves, scanning the dark leather spines. Finally, he pulled one out with a single gilt letter etched as a title. He set it on the desk in front of me. I had never read the volume before or even tugged it from its place. The pages were dark, not light as most parchment was, as rough and uneven as Lizzie's book.

On the front cover, crumbling with age, rose the golden outline of the Oakmaiden. Branch-arms outspread toward the heavens, her form was unmistakable. I opened to the first page, then the second. Flipping through, I saw that all the writing had been done in golden ink.

"That will give you something to decipher for a while," he said. "Maybe Neoma can help you. I've seen you two talking."

"This... this is exactly like my symbols," I breathed. The ink had the same shade, the same sheen. They were utterly identical. "Does the gold... Is the gold necessary for writing down the Oakmaiden's prophecies?"

Cal came closer to inspect the book and my shoulder. After a moment, he whistled. "The same ink! No wonder Endymion was so shaken when he saw." He shrugged. "I am just a soldier. And a friend. I don't know anything about historical prophecies and records and all those scholarly things."

"Is there someone who would know, that I could talk to?"

He leaned over my shoulder to spy at the frontispiece. "No author," he proclaimed. "There must be someone, but I don't know who. I'm sorry."

This felt important, as though I finally drew close to something that could matter. "That's all right. I'll find out." I stood as Cal moved to go. "Thank you for everything. It has meant so much to have a friend here."

The Fae turned. I still saw concern for Endymion written on his face, but his care encompassed me now too. "Little mortal," he said teasingly, "the King has been more hopeful these past few months than I've seen in decades. Perhaps I ought to thank you."

He held out a hand and I clasped it. I stumbled as he used the leverage to draw me in for a hug.

"Good luck in your endless investigation," he chuckled, turning to go. "Maybe you will find something new after all."

❧

THE BOOK SEEMED SO PRECIOUS THAT I WAS LOATHE TO TAKE IT from the library. I decided to leave it on the shelf where I could find it again once I tracked down someone who could help me interpret it.

Hunger eventually drew me to the dining room. A modest offering of tomatoes, pastry cups filled with a savory nut mixture, two kinds of hard cheeses, and herb-infused bread dusted with gold piled on the table. After consuming enough to stave off my hunger, I realized I had thought this feast normal. Was I forgetting my roots, my hard-working family struggling to offer so much as a dish of beans for supper? I hated to think I'd grown spoiled in in the midst of such opulence, even here in the lower level where the wealth and grandeur of above were muted.

Neoma knew of no scribe for the Oakmaiden's prophecies, so I was forced to look elsewhere. Ellis might be my best choice, but she had made it clear how much she disliked me.

"Oh!" I exclaimed after colliding with someone as I rounded a corner. Determination fueled my quick steps. "I'm sorry."

A strong hand cupped my shoulder, straightening me.

It was Endymion.

Far from his messy appearance last night, he stood in new leathers, his bronze skin without a blemish, gold once again adorning his ears to a point. I immediately remembered the feel of him from last night. Today he looked a decadent king, strong and magical enough to fear nothing, his sensual mouth inviting wickedness. Our experience in the pool was impossible. His golden regard was alien.

"I think this might be it," he said in an urgent undertone.

And he was End again. He seemed elated, ablaze with purpose.

"A solution at last."

"Calyse told me you had discovered something," I said. "I might have, too."

Glancing around, he guided me down the hall to one of the locked doors. This metal handle looked like a pair of birds. He produced a small key, seemingly from nowhere, and let us in. I'd passed this door a hundred times without knowing what it was. Light already shone inside, though not much. It illuminated lines of barrels, shelves of bottles, and various pitchers, some like huge vases, others metal or glass, still others tall and thin as aspen trees. An earthy sweet-sharp scent permeated the air. It made me think of the feast I'd come upon in the woods, when I'd almost eaten fairy fruit. The smell alone left me pleasantly lightheaded.

"A cave north of Realt is being guarded by a legion of dark creatures under Im Scathail's command."

"You mean, he can work independent of you?"

"They're... loyal to the Enemy," he revised.

It wasn't an answer exactly, but I nodded. Interesting to think that Im Scathail's shadows and power weren't located only inside Endymion. Despite the idea of "dark creatures", that gave me a little hope.

"I think what I need is there." His sensual lips curved. "This could be the different ending I desired, one that finally quenches despair."

Recalling Calyse's tentative expression, I pressed, "What do you think is there?"

"The Ash of Primilu."

I returned his gaze, but the name meant nothing to me.

Seeing my confusion, he licked his lips and explained, "She's a tree of legend. I did not know whether she still existed in reality."

I pictured a being much like the Oakmaiden. "And you think she will grant you freedom from this curse?"

"If the Ash of Primilu is there, she is the most powerful possibility I've encountered since..." His eyes went dark.

"The Great Sleep," I supplied.

"Yes."

It didn't escape me that Endymion was finally sharing his plans with me directly. Before, he had gone on trips or travels or missions, but with nothing definitive for me to picture what he was doing. Had last night changed all that? It seemed foolish to hold onto that hope among immortal beings.

"And your news?" His voice was clipped but genuinely curious. A few tiny drops of what looked like blood sprayed his hand as he gestured to me.

"Where were you just now?" I asked, distracted by the stains.

"Holding court." Catching my look, he added, "Fae existence cannot brook liars and destroyers of others."

The fawn boy, whom I hadn't thought about in ages, suddenly sprang to mind. He had been trying to poison me to present some misguided gift to the King, but his eyes were soft and his antlers beautiful.

I tried to shut out the memory. The Fae were volatile in every story, quick to violence, quick to love, luxuriating in extravagance. I understood now where the rumors came from, but I also saw their limitations.

"I... discovered that the paint on my shoulder matches the writing in a book of prophecies given by the Oakmaiden." An idea struck. "Do you know the scribe?"

"Zuca is the Oakmaiden's scribe, though she is ancient." He peered questioningly at me. "What do you expect to find from her?"

"I'm not certain. I have questions about all the prophecies. Perhaps hidden within them is a solution, in case you need another."

I thought for a moment he was about to kiss me again. My body responded, rushing with heat, tingling with the knowledge that we were alone.

"Pursue whatever you wish," he said huskily, "but I believe the ash may hold the cure. I must go and make preparations. You do the same."

He opened the door to the hallway once more.

I prayed he was right, but set off to find Zuca the scribe nonetheless.

I had to seek out Ellis after all. She eyed me warily, but accompanied me to the upper level where I could inquire about the location of Zuca the scribe. For centuries, she had written down the Oakmaiden's prophecies in gold ink, so I had many questions to ask her.

"It is irreverent to trouble the seer and her worker," Ellis informed me.

No one had said as much when I visited the Oakmaiden the first time, so I tried to dismiss her words as officious. "Endymion doesn't mind that I see them," I replied.

She shot a look at me, obviously taken aback at my casual defiance.

After asking several beings over the course of nearly the entire day, a rabbit-like forest creature claimed to know Zuca's assistant. We followed that trail—Ellis profoundly irritated by now but still clinging to me with the persistence of fur on an animal—and ended up in a part of the castle I'd never seen before. It was narrow and low-ceilinged, unlike most of the spaces aboveground. Little gold or precious stone adorned its walls. Instead it looked old and almost homely. I wondered if the castle had incorporated this structure into it when the building was erected, much like the special room had been made to accommodate the Oakmaiden herself. As we continued down the hall, it became a tunnel. I hadn't noticed the shift, but the change from wood and metal to rugged rock now alarmed me.

I looked at Ellis for confirmation that we hadn't wandered into a dangerous area, but she merely strode beside me, regal and aloof as ever. Thinking of the blood on Endymion's hands, I mused that nowhere in the Other Kingdom was truly safe.

Collecting my courage, I forged ahead. The air smelled like wet stone. Almost at the end of the tunnel, lit by candles in simple metal sconces, a carved opening revealed a little room.

Ellis and I turned right to see what was inside. I immediately felt as though I had shrunk. A well-appointed, burrow-like space had moss the color of autumn leaves covering the center of the floor like a rug. Holes in the rock held scrolls and books, some crammed on top of one another, others delicately positioned alone. A small chandelier of antlers covered in red and cream-colored wax drippings hung over a circular table with stout legs. At the table, eating a mushroom sandwich with thin, knobby fingers, sat an ancient mouse-like creature.

Her tiny black eyes squinted up warily at our entrance. Patchy gray fur covered her face and the exposed parts of her neck and hands. She wore a shawl over dark brown linen. Beside the crumbs of her sandwich were a mess of black and golden inkwells. The very table looked like a piece of art. Long-dried ink undulated and dripped and flowed across the tabletop. Stacks of black and white parchment framed the copper plate where the ancient mouse woman now set her meal.

She made a noise that was certainly speaking, but in no

language that I knew. Her tone, however, as quavery as it was, still revealed suspicion.

Ellis responded in an offhanded way. I realized they were both speaking in the Fae tongue. It had sounded so strange in the creature's mouth that I hadn't even recognized it.

"I see," the creature hissed, turning her attention to me.

"Are you Zuca?" I asked, though the answer was clear enough.

Her head twitched downward impatiently.

"I am Laura of Selene."

No acknowledgment met this announcement. The accusatory stare practically shouted that I was only a human who could have no business there.

"I am engaged to King Endymion."

Zuca smacked her furry lips meditatively. I saw a skinny tail slither around to one side of the table. Her aspect seemed to proclaim that I had gained enough clout to speak.

"I'm here to learn about the prophecies you write down from the Oakmaiden."

"You have access to her yourself. What need have you of me?" Zuca's reedy voice bore the weight of centuries.

"I want to know all the prophecies pertaining to the war against Im Scathail, and I want to know how the prophecies are produced."

Zuca leapt up from her little stool and bustled to the wall where a chaotic stack of black scrolls had been stuffed into the wall. She stood only as high as my chin, and even lower than that on Ellis.

"You want to know much," she grumbled, running her thin, nail-tipped fingers over the scroll caps.

"Does she come up with them herself, or does she receive her wisdom from elsewhere?"

At this, Zuca said something to Ellis in Fae. After a brief, no doubt derisive, conversation, Zuca finally responded to me.

"The Oakmaiden is the source. She has no need of elsewhere." She selected a thick scroll and pulled it out. The cylinder stood nearly as tall as her. "This is the compilation, categorized by subject."

I reached out to take it.

Zuca drew back. "The document is not to leave the room of records!" she snapped. "Greedy human..."

To my surprise, Ellis stood forward. "You would address your future queen in such a way?" Her lip curled in a way reminiscent of her son. "Disrespect her again if you wish to lose your tail. I see no purpose it would serve in your work."

The ancient mouse-creature drew her bald tail around herself protectively, although her pinched expression was sour.

I looked gratefully at Ellis, but she did not look back. Apparently, some disdain for me was allowed, but Zuca had stepped over the line. Ellis' defense of me, distant though she was, meant more to me than the effusive congratulations of all the subjects at the engagement party.

"Look here, please," said Zuca in a brittle tone, placing the scroll on the little painted table and rolling it open.

I recognized the handwriting from the black book in Endymion's library. All the words here were written in gold as well. I found the symbols matching those on my shoulder almost instantly. I'd spent so much time combing the records for them that I knew them as well as human writing. The rest, however, might as well have been miniaturized child's drawings.

Ellis began translating them for me, one by one. Such and such a battle would be won by a rowen tree and a white ewe, a long-ago general would lose his life after two blood moons...

I lost track of time in the little cave. Most of the prophecies were so obscure or rooted to things that had already happened that nothing seemed immediately helpful. My hand balled into a fist on the tabletop. Why could I do so little to assist those I cared about? Was I doomed merely to be a pawn in greater matters? I had honestly thought I'd find answers here.

The glass domed ceiling showed it was night by the time I went back to the lower level, stiff and disheartened. Endymion was gone. Hopefully he was right and the ash would provide him the cure he needed, because I could offer him no alternative if he failed.

🙟   25   🙠

The next few week passed in a blur. I received my morning baths and I slept longer than usual, which reminded me unpleasantly of Calyse's blessing.

I didn't know where to turn next. Nothing I did could help Endymion or Lizzie or anyone else. Without End, I had no public appearances to attend. Ellis remained, but she would not let me explore the upper floors alone. I felt, once again, like a prisoner.

One week became two, and I started to wonder about Endymion. The cave he spoke of could be far away. Not every mission was only one day's ride away, I told myself. And besides, he was a mighty Fae, not a mere human. My worry was unfounded.

Still, a dread I couldn't shake coated me more thickly with every passing day.

🙟🙠

SUDDENLY, FOR APPARENTLY NO REASON AT ALL, I BOLTED awake. The silken sheets fell to my lap as I listened for whatever it was that had roused me. Nothing but the crackle of the fire and the churn of water in the dark.

Then I heard it.

Footsteps, much louder than I was used to, and, faintly, screams. The panicked shouts cut off, not as though the people had stopped, but as though a door had been closed.

Something was happening in the upper level.

I grabbed the fluffy robe by my bedside and ran outside. Endymion always returned via the lower level so no one would see his comings and goings. Did someone know he was gone and so threatened the main part of the castle?

The screams grew louder in the hallway. The door to the upper floor had been opened again. Squeals and cries of horror and the shouted names of loved ones pierced my heart.

I barely sensed my own body, so hot and cold, light and heavy it was.

It would be safer down here. I knew I ought to stay, but I had to know what was going on. Why was everyone in such a panic?

Stumbling on numb legs, I climbed the steps. The sight made my throat close in horror.

Billowing to the ceiling far above, black as smoke, shadows rolled through the enormous room. Fae and forest creatures disappeared within the surging cloud, their eyes bulging with terror just before they fell out of sight. Many ran toward me, trying for the stairs. Before they could reach them, the Shadow enveloped us all.

I was blind, my surroundings black as pitch. Instead of the suffocating sensation I expected, the darkness only brought cold and touches like a hundred fingers, though none of them coiled and grasped like those in my room. Occasionally they plucked at my clothes or slid in a sinister way down my skin. I could hear others still conscious, crying or calling out.

"Have you seen...?"

"...the Great Sleep."

"Im Scathail!"

"I can't..."

"The Oakmaiden's been—"

I whipped my head in the direction of the final voice. "The Oakmaiden's been what?" I demanded.

Wailing met my question. My blood chilled. That probably meant...

I ran blindly in the general direction of the Rose Room. In some places the shadows were thin enough that I could see a step or two ahead. I redirected my steps and kept running. More than once I collided with another being.

Soon, the shouting became a faintly positive sign. The Shadow wasn't killing or putting everyone to sleep this time. Hopefully it wasn't maiming anyone either.

Invisible fingers pulled at me but I kept running. Through a shredding of fog I saw the Rose Room ahead, its interior even blacker than its surroundings. The doors were wide open. I plunged inside.

I stifled the urge to cough in the complete darkness, but these shadows only moved like smoke. They didn't burn acrid like smoke. I felt them touch me, blowing my face cold, fingers catching in my hair. I shuddered. There hadn't been so great a moving wave of darkness outside as I sensed here.

This was the source.

Pressing on, I reached the Oakmaiden's chamber. A pale glimmer made me step to the side for a reprieve from the darkness, but what I saw ripped a scream from me.

The Oakmaiden had been torn with great black rents as though struck by lightning. Whole branches lay strewn on the ground and her torso had split in two. One half remained upright but twisted unnaturally as though writhing in agony. The other half crashed down against the circular opening in the ground, still partially attached to the trunk. I felt sick looking at her.

Slowly, I rounded the space behind where her stately form had once stood. Shadows gushed from the side opposite me, flowing in a current out the door and into the concourse. The sight was unholy—blackness streaming thickly into the air, some of it curling around the remains of the Oakmaiden on its terrorizing way.

Finally, I saw him.

Until that moment, I hadn't admitted to myself what I thought I would find.

Endymion.

He lay curled on his side, unconscious, one side of him impossible to see for the shadows rushing out of him. But I saw the curl of his hair, the side of his neck, his broad shoulders, and I knew.

"End!" I knelt beside him, the darkness like cold river water beneath my hand when I touched him. "Endymion!"

He didn't stir.

"End, stop this!" I screamed. Gripping his shoulder, I rolled him onto his back.

His chest had been slashed open. Gouts of blood ran from the wound.

"Oh!" My hands flew to my mouth. "Endymion! Endymion!" I touched his face. It was cold.

Was he even alive? That wound looked nasty and he wasn't moving.

I knew nothing about the differences between humans and Fae, but I assumed that living beings had to have a pulse. I shoved two fingers under his neck. Right beside my hand, darkness streamed from him. I thought I might be sick.

There. A pulse. A strong pulse.

"Im Scathail!" I shouted. "Get out of him!"

I don't know what I thought would happen. Ancient beings didn't fear me. But the darkness hiccupped, like smoke being fanned by a blanket.

"Come back," I said more quietly, close to Endymion's face. After one more shake of his shoulder, I kissed him.

The shadows, to my amazement, became more intermittent. After swirling around me, catching my hair in a whirlwind, they coughed like a dying fire. After a few more seconds, all that was left were the shadows I'd seen several times before, caressing the King like smoke on a burning corpse.

I hadn't noticed the roar of the shadows until it was gone. Unearthly silence blanketed the violent scene in the Oakmaiden's room.

Endymion looked for all the world like a wounded soldier returning from the brink of death.

"End?"

He finally cracked open bloodshot eyes. "You're safe," he croaked, gazing up at me with a kind of horrified elation. "You're not..."

He turned his head to take in the rest of the scene. At first his carved face went expressionless, then he began to shake violently.

Did his wound hurt him?

His hand became a fist and he smashed it on the ground, rotating away from me. I heard his ragged gasps, his repeated curses. His back shuddered.

"Did I...?" Panting breaths cut off his ability to finish the question.

"Everyone else is alive, I think," I said in a hoarse whisper. "Not asleep either."

He seemed to deflate. "I am the Shadow," he breathed. "I'm Im Scathail."

"He used you."

"Were you the King," he spat, breathless, sitting up as though his chest wound were only an annoyance, "would you let me live?" His golden eyes roamed to the dismembered figure of the Oakmaiden.

I didn't know how to answer.

He dipped a finger in his own blood. "I would slice him open before the assembly and bathe the floor in his blood." The ferocity of his words took me aback. He looked every inch the wild Fae King he was. "It's only because I loved my own skin that I put my people at risk for so long." He smeared his fingertip meditatively across the stone floor. "The ash..." His eyes glistened with angry tears.

"It's not your fault." My words were barely audible as I ventured touching his shoulder.

He caught my hand in a tight grip. "It is. I should be slaughtered like the unholy beast I am." The fire seemed to die in his eyes. He looked younger, his lips parted in fear and determination.

I couldn't argue with him. He released my hand. If End died, perhaps Lizzie could be restored to her former state and the Shadow wouldn't threaten Selene or the Other Kingdom.

But I couldn't bear the thought.

My attention roamed back to the broken body of the Oakmaiden. Tears welled as I took in the ravaged branches. There was the one with the shard missing.

An idea blossomed, sharp and unexpected.

I turned my burning face to his. "Would you go on one more mission with me first?"

"Let's go. Now!" I urged. "Bandage yourself and let's go."

Fueled by some force I didn't understand, Endymion stood. Blood dripped from his chest to the floor. Perhaps the wound was only superficial. It didn't seem to slow him.

"Oh, little thorn, you make me hate myself."

I smiled despite his words and took his hand as he ran past the broken Oakmaiden in the opposite direction of the shadows.

The smoke and yelling persisted outside, though the darkness had become visibly thinner. I wasn't familiar with this part of the castle. It was so vast and I'd barely had the opportunity to see any of it.

End's jaw clenched tight beside me. He moved with the predatory grace of an animal, as though the castle were part of him.

We stayed to closed-in spaces, not the huge arcades. After a few twists and halls and staircases we reached a set of huge double doors with a metal frieze spanning both of them. A couple, clearly Fae for their beauty, fought against a cloudlike army in the top panel. In the bottom panel the same couple, or so I assumed, lounged naked on a large divan among a feast of plenty. Peace and war.

End pulled open the doors. I knew immediately what this was. His official bedchamber. All those weeks I had assumed he slept in the lower level, but that had to be only for emergencies. I'd been foolish to assume otherwise.

I had thought my room lavish. Endymion's bedroom had architecture within it, highlighting and differentiating different portions with grand arches and pillars carved like trees. Rich, gauzy fabrics flowed from the ceiling and around the huge bed, which stood on a marble dais. Fire stood on tall golden stands shaped like male and female figures. Food and drink and pleasures of all kinds adorned the space everywhere I looked. It took my breath away.

Endymion stripped off his clothes and headed over to a wash-basin beside a dark, sunken pool, which was much larger and more secluded than mine. He sponged off his bleeding chest, eyes tightly shut as though trying to forget what had happened. But there would be no forgetting. If his people found out that this was not simply an attack by Im Scathail, but that the shadows emanated from the King, there would be terror followed by mutiny.

The cut was shallow, as I'd hoped, though his whole body and the discarded clothes were covered in blood.

He had been so hopeful that his mission would work this time. He'd fought—that much was clear—and yet his failure reached beyond himself to grasp everyone he knew with evil, searching fingers.

He was the Shadow. Even without that, he was wild and untamed. I watched the muscles slide under the skin of his back as he washed himself off, and I couldn't help but be impressed. He fastened a makeshift bandage over the wound.

Without turning to me, he said, "What will I need? Armor? A suit?"

"A suit. We aren't going anywhere dangerous."

He pulled one from the wardrobe without asking any more questions. I felt aghast that he would follow my direction so blindly. Mine. Only a mortal.

The simple motions of dressing seemed to calm him. He buttoned the front with precision and checked each item to make sure it suited his liking. Everything was black. He washed his face and hair before fastening on the golden ear cuffs.

Finally, he turned around. "Is this suitable?"

I thought he looked gorgeously wicked, but I only said, "Yes."

"Shall I ready horses?"

"Yes, we're riding to Selene."

His brow quirked, but his business-like composure didn't break. I saw the pain in his eyes and knew he wore this cold mask so he could place one foot before the other.

"That golden brush," I explained. "I think it might be a piece of the Oakmaiden. And the golden ink looks exactly like her scribe's ink. Zuca told me that the Oakmaiden created the prophecies herself. She didn't draw them from another source. What if we could use that piece of her to create a new prophecy for ourselves?"

"You think it's the shard?" Life had begun to glow in his face again. I could almost see his heart beating faster.

"I don't know how it got there, but I do. Why else would the charm not come off me here? Why else would it have been found with a book of spells—well, we thought they were spells—that were really her prophecies? Why golden ink?"

The slightest smile curved End's mouth. "Well done, little thorn."

As sure as I was about my theory, doubts crawled over me like beetles. Endymion would put himself to death if this final trial didn't produce results, freeing him from the shadows for good. No matter how certain I felt, the weight of the consequences, should this fail, could crush me.

With clipped movements, End crossed the floor and headed out. Minutes later, I couldn't tell how—it felt almost like magic—we were in a grand stable. Once again, the ceilings were of an enormous height. Every amenity a horse or stablehand could need for sport or war lined one wall. The other wall housed large horses, mostly pure black or white.

End approached the nearest black horse. I recognized it from the night I'd wandered into the forest. He clucked to it and the horse responded, lowering its massive head against the King's.

"We'll ride together," he announced.

I wasn't a great rider, so the decision pleased me. He opened the stall door and the stallion clopped proudly out on feathered hooves.

I stepped back to allow End space to saddle the horse, but he beckoned me forward. When I stood before him, he lifted me up by my waist to straddle the stallion's broad back. It was as though I weighed nothing.

He mounted behind me and I felt the beast respond immediately to every shift, every soft sound Endymion made. I slid down until I was flush against his chest.

"I'm not hurting you?" I muttered, unable, for some reason, to speak more clearly.

"Pain can be pleasure too," he replied.

With a rush of wind, the black horse galloped out of the

stable, taking us into the night toward Selene, where I would pass once more beyond the barrier.

The night was as black as End's shadows.

Everything felt surreal. Autumn air whipped through my hair as Endymion guided the black stallion through the forest toward my village.

I hadn't seen it in months. Mother must have thought Lizzie and I had perished or been taken. The last would be correct. My heart broke for the pain all the generations of women in my family must have endured at the news. Guilt threaded through my chest as well. Should I have tried harder at the beginning to escape?

Even as I thought it, the shame dispelled. I couldn't have escaped, even if I had tried, and, if I had succeeded, Endymion would now be dead.

Creating a new prophecy had to work. End was serious when he said he would rather die than allow the Shadow to continue terrorizing his subjects.

Without reins or saddle, I couldn't tell how he directed the horse, but it responded to every whim and tightening of muscle. They seemed to speak the same body language. I was unused to riding horses, so I simply held on, protected by Endymion behind me.

He pulled the beast up short. After a short scuffle of hooves in the leaves, the stallion settled.

"This is the edge of the barrier," the King whispered low in my ear.

I couldn't see anything through the moonless trees. The thought of going alone through the woods stoked my childhood fear.

"Are there no forest folk to misguide me?" I asked.

"I patrol the barrier's edge. If anyone tries to lay a finger on you, I'll kill them." He said this evenly, though a latent anger simmered beneath the surface. I felt it in his core.

He dismounted and carried me down next. The horse's head towered above me.

"I'll return with the brush and ink. And the book." I didn't know why I hesitated. Perhaps it was the thick veneer of dread pooling in my gut, the certainty that End would take no more chances. Would something as simple as a golden brush be enough?

"We'll be waiting."

I could just make out his tall form laying a big hand on the horse's back.

I headed toward the village of Selene, to my house, where Mother and Grandmother and Great-grandmother lived. I yearned to talk to them, but instead I was there to steal.

The barrier didn't begin deep in the forest, but on the outskirts. Soon, I saw faint lights fighting through the late-night darkness. There were Jonathan's barn, James' bakery, and just beyond them, the garden that I loved. And on the right sat my cottage.

In that moment, I missed Lizzie as deeply as I ever had. I never meant to return alone.

I pinched myself to bring my mind back to the task at hand. Our house was small and Grandmother in particular was a light sleeper. The golden brush lay in the room Lizzie and I shared, which meant I had to pass through the cramped living room.

Never before had our tiny house looked so shabby to me. Dried and shredded remains of dandelions still hung on the doorframe.

I held my breath tight in my lungs. Reaching silently for the handle, I turned it with little sound. I wished I had the Fae's supernatural quietness. A fire burned low in the hearth, gilding the silhouette of Great-grandmother in the chair. A lump stuck in my throat. I couldn't greet her, not now with so much at stake. They'd prevent me from ever leaving again, and I had to, right away.

The room belonging to me and Lizzie opened on the lefthand side of where I stood. I slipped in. All was dark and smelled of dust and cherries.

I felt blindly for the items I knew were there: the long wooden handle of the brush, the round pot of golden ink, and the old book of spells. They were awkward to hold without clattering one against the other.

The brush made a faint tap against the book's cover. I froze.

No sound came from the living room or the other bedroom. Then, a creak. Someone was moving. I backed further into the shadows, wondering if I could get out the window, then wondering why I hadn't tried that in the first place. One attempt showed me that the window didn't open wide enough to fit me, especially holding an awkward assortment of objects. So I waited.

Footsteps came into the living room. The front door opened and shut. The footsteps retreated. I knew that tread as my Mother's. I wanted to burst out, fling myself into her arms and tell her I was all right. Instead, I bit my lip and waited until she was safely back in bed before I fled the house and ran back into the forest.

My eyes had adjusted better to the darkness but I still stumbled over invisible things as I hurried back to Endymion. The forest didn't have landmarks like the village. Every young woman was warned so heartily to stay away from it that I had never gone into the Other Kingdom until the night I followed Lizzie.

I stifled a scream when I nearly collided with a large body. Endymion had appeared in front of me.

"Those are the items?" he asked.

"Yes." I handed them to him one by one.

He seemed to appraise them, though I couldn't make out any details in the darkness. It was then that I realized a snag in the plan. "I can't see well in the dark," I said. "I can't write what I can't see. We'll have to wait."

But Endymion didn't respond. His expression had frozen, head tilted down toward the old book of spells. He looked like a statue of Death.

"Is... something wrong?" I asked.

He rubbed his thumb over the book's cover. I made out a faint exhale. Straining to see what he was staring at, I pivoted so I could look from the same angle he did. It was still too black for me to distinguish specific features. My memory of the cover didn't suggest anything shocking.

"Rose," he breathed, throaty with longing.

Then I remembered that in the corner of the cover, there was a faint capital R, a scratched initial I hadn't considered important before. The book had passed down through generations of my family, after all. I assumed one of the book's previous owners had scratched her initial there.

"Was this her book?" I asked haltingly.

"It belonged to my library. It disappeared around the time we first feared..." Reverently, he opened the pages. "She always did say that humans could help our cause. I didn't believe her. She was the only exception."

My heart beat thickly, painfully. I wanted to be an exception too. "You still love her." It was both a statement and question.

"Of course. Our souls were one. I never could have been taken by the Shadow without her destruction." His tone turned dangerously bitter.

"Her sacrifice to the Enemy?" I clarified.

"We were prepared for the sting of victory but not the sting of defeat." He sighed and closed the book. "You're much like her, little thorn."

He said the words meditatively but they still made my heart leap. A new idea had started forming in my mind. "Could that soul connection," I began cautiously, "have worked in the opposite direction? Away from the shadows?"

"You don't know what you speak of."

"I know. But could it? If Rose hadn't sacrificed herself, could your bond have been strong enough to save you?"

"She was strong enough to drink starlight and dance the trees bare."

Shivers washed down my body.

"She should not have loved a wicked king."

His words took me aback.

"I think we should try it." Had the woods not been so quiet, I wouldn't have heard myself.

"Try? What?"

"I think... just in case... that we should marry as the prophecy says."

"Impossible," he growled.

"If there's an extra chance you can survive, free from the shadows—"

"I said I would try one more thing. Have I not accommodated you?"

His tone stung. "Well then," I said, "unless you have a lantern, I must wait for first light to use the golden brush, and that's hours away. Is there a place we can rest until then?" I swallowed down the pain in my throat.

"You forget who you're speaking to," he said, with almost apologetic gentleness.

Tiny flames, like fireflies, bloomed in the trees, the bushes, and among the leaves littering the forest floor, revealing a finer hollow than the one I'd stumbled across the first time. The black stallion chomped grasses just outside the circle of light.

Awestruck, I entered. "I didn't know you could do that," I breathed.

"Fae Kings have many talents and no need to display them all at once." He seemed more like himself than he had a moment ago. "Laura."

I turned away from gazing at the magical sight of the hollow to look at him. Book, ink, and brush lay in a pile near his feet.

He stood gazing down at me with a painful intensity. "I cannot marry you. I've already told you the reason."

I would destroy you eventually.

I took in his despair, his beauty, his burden. "*Could* it help?" I asked again.

He didn't dismiss me right away this time, but considered. "Theoretically, it might. But it couldn't work between us."

"Why not?"

"It has to be a marriage of love, not duty."

I felt as though he'd struck me. The implication had been

strong, but confirmation stabbed. "I'm sorry I couldn't be enough," I finally managed.

A line formed between his brows. He caught me as I bent to retrieve the golden brush, placing both his hands on my shoulders. "I am the monster, little thorn," he said, regarding me with confusion. "My shadows will consume you. I know there is no way, no matter how wide your compassion, that you could love a king of death."

I stared up at him, lips trembling. My mouth went totally dry. "But I do."

He canted his head suspiciously. "If I thought that," he said slowly, voice rich and deep, "I'd bathe you in diamonds, bring mountains down on anyone who belittled you..." He stopped, his breath catching.

My stomach flipped dizzyingly.

He licked his tantalizing lower lip. "Perhaps... I should make you queen, for the end, because I love you too, Laura of Selene."

$\maltese$ 28 $\maltese$

My skin tingled with Endymion's earnest pronouncement that, impossibly, he loved me. How could I have inspired such obsession in a handsome, powerful king?

My face flushed. I longed to kiss him, but I tried to keep my head. The materials for a new prophecy lay at our feet, and a marriage could provide possible insurance if anything went wrong. And if both measures failed...

I couldn't allow myself to think about it. Endymion had made clear that he would, for the sake of his kingdom, order himself to death.

"What is necessary for a Fae marriage?" I asked in a breathy voice, hoping a large crowd or something else left in Tylaith Castle wouldn't be required. "The minimum."

"A living witness, two vows, and consummation."

I felt drunk with the last word but I said, "Living witness?"

He gestured to the large trees around us. They, I realized, were living.

"And the... vows?"

"I will repeat the words to you."

We both seemed spellbound, speaking mechanically, making no move toward one another.

"Shall we do it before writing a new prophecy?" I asked.

A fleeting moment of intense sorrow and regret passed over his face. No doubt the image of the ravaged Oakmaiden filled his mind then. I touched his forearm to bring him back to the present.

"I won't let anything happen to you," he said fiercely, without answering the question.

"I know," I said. But there were no guarantees. I was willing to risk myself if it meant his freedom and the defeat of Im Scathail.

He took a few slow breaths before cutting a glance at me. "Are you sure you want to do this? You may love me somehow, but you know what I am. You can still change your mind. I will not mourn in your presence."

In answer, I slipped my fingers through his long, callused ones. "I want you whole."

His answering look was devouring. He squeezed my hand in the candlelit hollow and together we faced a great oak. Endymion's black horse was a second witness.

Words began to spill from the King's lips, delicious, unknown words with passion in them. I struggled to remember the sounds. The forest itself seemed to sigh in response when he finished.

Turning to me, he repeated the words very slowly. I tasted them in my own mouth, feeling the truth of them, though not the sense.

"Let it be," he murmured after I'd reached the conclusion of my vow. He caught and held my gaze. "I vow with blood and mind and bone my troth to thee. I pledge, come hell or heaven, to knit my soul with yours in love, to champion and protect. My life is yours, my body is yours, from this moment unto death."

I had known the words, although I hadn't understood them. I repeated them in my own tongue, feeling strangely inadequate next to the Fae King's imposing form. Orange flame glittered on his golden ear cuffs.

The ceremony had lasted only five minutes, but it left me breathless.

"My queen," he said and bowed his head, his lashes fluttering closed.

"My king." My whole body felt warm and alight.

Without more speech, we surged together, desperate to taste, to feel. His soft lips moved over mine, insistent, possessive, while his large hands cradled my back.

I threaded fingers through his dark hair, scraping his scalp with my nails. The motion drew a moan from him that quickened my pulse everywhere.

He ripped the dress as he yanked it off my body. I stood exposed in the cool wind before him. He didn't let me remain cool for long. Falling to his knees, he gripped my waist and pulled me to him, sucking each nipple, one at a time, hard into his mouth. I gasped. He laved my breasts with his tongue as though I were the most delectable fairy fruit.

In a swift motion, he stood and swung me into his arms, setting me softly on a bed of moss and leaves. His eyes were dark with need when he looked at me, frantically undoing the buttons on his immaculate suit jacket, then the shirt, the boots, the trousers. My landscape became only ridged bronze skin slashed through with a thin bandage.

I lifted one knee, inviting him down with me. He needed no such invitation. My entire body demanded him, wrapping around his hips and arching closer. His hard muscles and teasing hands made me slick for him. I needed him inside me, to take full possession of me.

"Please," I begged.

Endymion growled and guided himself to my entrance. I bucked my hips to take him in. His eyes rolled back as though my insistence gave him painful pleasure.

"Please," I repeated, cheeks hot, hands searching the divots of his lower back to press him more firmly into me.

Finally, I cried out as he slid in, though not far.

"Ooh," he grunted. "You're tight, little thorn."

"I'm sorry."

"No," he breathed hot against my ear. "No apologies. This way I get to open you wider." His voice was sinful.

I strained against the wet pressure between my legs.

His slow whisper was as delicious as sucking cocoa from a hot mug. "I imagined you as a feast. I would lick between your legs and suck hard on your nipples." He ran a rough thumb over one of them.

I inhaled sharply, arching further. He pushed farther in.

His hand traveled down my stomach to my wet, aching clit. He pressed down with two fingers and made hard rhythmic circles. My inner muscles shuddered and he slid in farther. I whimpered at the building ecstasy, the incessant cry of *more, more, more*.

"And you would scream with pleasure and beg me for more." His voice was a rumble. He bit my earlobe.

I cried out and let him in farther. A scream scratched at my throat, trying for release.

"I want every noise," he grunted, pressing in all the way, "every bite, every scream—"

My head threw back in a sharp yell. I hardly knew where I was, only knew the Fae King on top of me, his muscles moving under my hands, his hips rolling into me, his fingers rubbing the nub between my legs.

His thrusts became quicker, more demanding. Groans erupted from him. His wet fingers gripped my shoulder as though he needed to hang onto something. "I won't... be able... to last," he panted.

I whimpered and writhed, only encouraging his need. He gave a few hard thrusts and I couldn't hold back. Releasing every inhibition over to pleasure, I screamed. We came together.

Hearts pounding, covered in sweat, we rolled apart. His hair was a tangle, his lips swollen. He scooped me close for another kiss, sucking at my bottom lip when he pulled away. Gazing at me through hooded lids, his mouth twisted in a smirk. I was speechless at how beautiful he was.

My wicked king.

❧ 29 ❧

unlight leaked through the trees before we were done with each other, and even then, urgency required us to think of other things. Endymion vexed and satisfied me as no one else could. He was desperate, hungry, as though this would be his last chance to taste me, to make me feel unbound.

I hoped that wasn't true.

We sat together, exhausted and sore, against the trunk of a gigantic tree, peering at the book I'd grown up with.

"Time to write a new ending," the King murmured, capturing pieces of my wayward blonde hair that had fallen and tucking it back in place.

In the fervor of the past few hours, I'd forgotten to worry about the new prophecy. Did one require special wording to work? Was writing it enough, or should we also speak it aloud?

I wished I had asked Zuca so many more questions.

"You can read these," I said, trailing my finger along the golden symbols on the page. "How do you think ours should begin?"

"As we have." His golden-eyed gaze darted playfully to me. He kissed an apology for the suggestion on my bare shoulder. "We should amend the standing prophecy," he said, as though he'd thought so for some time.

"And say what?"

"*If she would wed the King, all war against the Enemy will cease,*" he recited. "*And the Enemy will be destroyed.*"

"Maybe it is more powerful to add onto the Oakmaiden's words," I agreed. "Is there any way that ending could twist itself, though?" I disliked the possibility that End could be swept away along with Im Scathail.

"*And the Enemy alone,*" he amended.

I preferred that version. I nodded.

"*The King's mortal bride shall outlive all her kind and remain the fascination of her husband always.*" His expression softened. Morning light washed his naked form with gold. "No sacrifice."

"Of you either," I said, caressing his neck. "But is that too long an amendment?"

"Two sentences at the behest of the King of the Fae shouldn't be an imposition." The authority rumbling behind his words made me shiver.

I took up the golden brush. "On paper?"

"On skin," he purred. "Always more powerful." He plucked the brush from me.

"You'll have to direct me how to do the letters," I said.

"Or where," he teased, squaring himself so he faced my shoulder, the one with writing already on it. Uncapping the bottle of ink, he dipped the soft bristles in. Never before had that ink looked so like liquid gold as it did now, in this hollow. With a cool slide across my skin, the brush moved with sure strokes. Endymion's face burned with intensity as he formed each perfect letter. The new words glided behind my arm, up to my nape, and down the column of my spine. Each line was a precise caress.

When he finished, he blew on the damp ink, planting kisses along the length of the sentences.

I released a breath as I rotated to take my turn. I'd have to write more on him, I realized, because he didn't already have part of the prophecy tattooed. I couldn't help running my hand lightly down his well-muscled arm before I began.

"Now, now," he tutted. "No touching until you're done."

It took all my willpower not to give him a spiteful kiss. Focusing once more on the book lying open beside us, I located the original words written on me. Starting there, I copied them with as much precision as I could onto his shoulder, as it was written on mine.

"Very good. I'll show you the next letters." He paused. "It will be easier if you do them on the front for me."

I had to be so close to his skin to write properly that I ended up straddling him, my eye contact defying him to comment. I knew I was wet and I knew he could tell. A smile spread over his face. "That will do, little thorn." He took my non-dominant hand and forced it to the soft ground. "Here's how it begins." Singling out one of my fingers, he drew a figure in the dirt. I slowly copied his motion until a radiant letter stood out against his bronze skin.

"And another." He made my finger draw a strong, circular shape. I steadied my writing hand and followed suit.

"New word."

We went on like that until his words trailed down in a mirror image of mine, straight down the planes of his chest and just past his navel. As he had done, I blew on the words to dry them.

"Now what do we do?" I asked.

After a flicker of mischief, his demeanor turned serious. "We say them. We chant them. We will them into being."

"Teach me."

Just as he had the previous night, End walked me through the sounds until I could hobble through them on my own. There was a music in them.

End spoke our new prophecy first. He stood, glorious and unashamed as an ancient god, and ordered these things to be.

My contribution was just as important. Standing beside him, I declared our new intention.

A slight breeze cut through the hollow, but there was nothing supernatural in it. No darkness thundered. The earth didn't quake. There was no way to know if my scheme had worked.

We shucked on our discarded clothes, but only after one final joining. I touched him in many ways I wanted to, and there were still many more. He lingered with me, learning what made me knife backward with a strangled scream and trying to prolong my release. He already knew my body as if he'd spent months exploring it. I recognized what Orlando did to Genevieve.

But we couldn't live in the hollow. We had to return to the castle, the King and Queen of the Fae.

❧

I HOPED IT WAS A TRICK OF THE LIGHT. ON OUR WAY BACK TO Tylaith Castle, Endymion's form blurred a little. A slight curl of steam here, a shadow there.

We were in a forest full of innocent shadows, I reasoned. And he could be warm and steaming in the cool air. I'd seen workers' heads steaming in winter before. Why not the King's arms wrapping me in place?

By the time we reached the stable, a different one than before, he was muttering to himself—something in Fae. It sounded memorized.

I was not comforted.

He eased me onto the straw-strewn ground and kissed my forehead. "You still prefer to stay filthy, I see," he said.

My dress had torn significantly the night before. It hung on me like rags now, barely decent. Dirt and leaves embedded themselves in our hair. We looked bruised and feral.

I watched as the column of his neck moved in a swallow. I, too, was fighting off another bolt of desire. Time was against us. Now, we had to face the aftermath of the Shadow attack and see if my plan worked. Was End free or not?

"Get cleaned up," he said, deep enough that I felt his voice in my chest. "I can't present you as queen like this. Only I get to see you this way." His look became molten but unreadable. He stared at me a moment before reaching up to his ear. Releasing one golden ornament, he cupped my ear with it, giving it a non-human point at the top. The metal felt warm from the heat of his skin. Now we each wore one cuff.

"I love you," I said.

"Until death." He gave me a final lingering kiss. "I'll send for your belongings to be moved to the royal suite. Until then, your room is that way. Go straight until the second staircase. The door to the hallway will be unlocked." He seemed preoccupied. Perhaps the inevitable fallout over the Oakmaiden's death worried him. It concerned me too, but I would be right by his side to face the difficulty together. If he was worried about the Shadow...

It wouldn't be long before I saw him again and could evaluate the success of our plan. He would be safe until then.

I laid a reassuring hand on his rough cheek before I left him alone.

❦ 30 ❦

I fastened the ear cuff in place last. Freshly cleaned, I emerged wearing my grandest gown, befitting a queen of the Fae. It was made of black silk with a deep neckline. A gold filigree collar attached to the gown with delicate hanging chains. The design on the neckpiece mirrored a starburst on the waist. Hung over my shoulders was a matching cape sporting braided gold epaulets on the broad shoulders.

I would match Endymion in his finest suit when he announced me.

But he wasn't waiting, as I had expected. Instead, I heard confused voices in the hall. My gut clenched. This felt too similar to when the Shadow had rushed out of End in a wave that threatened us all.

Tentatively, I stepped forward, listening. The voices weren't refined, like the Fae. They were all female, calling out or murmuring in dreadful confusion.

Could it be...?

My heart leapt. I ran toward the stoat room only to find the door open. Within, white-clad figures were sitting up, rubbing their faces, baring their teeth in confusion, like a congregation of ghosts. Some of the beds were empty, including Lizzie's. Where was my sister?

In a desperation of happiness, I spun to search for her. My plan had worked! The golden brush left in the hollow had forged a new ending for us all.

The Shadow's curse no longer bound Endymion. Free from possession, he could begin to mend, to forgive himself for the destruction wrecked by Im Scathail using him as a vessel.

Glad tears streamed down my face. At last, all would be well.

"Lizzie!" I cried. "Lizzie!"

I ran as quickly as I could through the labyrinthine passages. Phantoms of other girls passed by. "You're all right. You'll be all right," I said, although their faces were wasted and their eyes all burned yellow. Concern for them bubbled up inside me. Would they age quickly now that enchanted sleep did not protect them? Would their addiction continue? Could they be returned to their families in Selene?

"Laura?"

I whirled. From a side passage had come my sister. The white shift hung on her emaciated body. Even her cheeks had sunken in. Her blonde hair looked brittle, her lips white with dehydration, her pale hands like blue-veined stone, but what struck me most were her eyes. They glowed golden.

"Laura?" she croaked again.

"Lizzie!" I flung myself at her and kissed her gaunt face. For a moment I had almost forgotten she was taller than I, she looked so small. "Lizzie, I'll take care of you. I'm sorry I scolded you for choosing James. I understand now and I love you for it."

She stood oddly still while I embraced her, not the vivacious girl who had stormed into the woods that night.

"Where...?" she began.

Heavy footsteps—a sound I wasn't used to hearing in these halls—sounded behind us. I turned to see the dark figure of Calyse, head bowed, shoulders slumped forward, crossing a perpendicular hallway. His very aura spoke of something horrible.

My throat closed. I carefully took Lizzie's hand and guided her back toward Calyse.

"Cal!" I shouted.

Two nearby maidens lifted their listless heads.

"Cal, what's wrong?"

His expression when he finally faced me turned my bowels to ice. Every muscle strained in agony, not with the memory of horror, but the immediate presence of it. Blood covered his hands and showed as darker patches on his leather armor.

"Are you all right?" I demanded, rushing forward.

Calyse recoiled.

Then I saw the blood didn't come from him.

"What happened?" I breathed, but I feared I already knew the answer.

"It was his command. Even before we left. I vowed to him." The words were fierce but hardly audible. His lip trembled. "He... He told me to announce you as queen. Then you may do as you see fit." He dropped to one knee, a bloody fist against his chest.

Hot and cold warred senselessly within me. "Where is he?"

"Outside, near the stable."

I had only just left him when... Frantic, I charged back the way I had come. I couldn't move fast enough. I couldn't do enough. I should have known the moment I saw the maidens up and walking. The death of Im Scathail would negate the effect the fairy fruit, but not of their enchanted sleep. That mercy was Endymion's alone.

I could barely see by the time I yanked open the door leading to the stable. "End!" I screamed. "Endymion!"

All around me, through the stable and beyond, shadows were dissipating like fog, making it harder to see. I scanned the ground.

"End!" I opened the stable door and saw, lying crumpled on the ground within a circle of red oak leaves, my husband's body. Choking on a sob, I flew to him, collapsing to my knees. His beautiful face looked pale. He hadn't even washed since our ride through the forest. Blood still oozed from a deep wound through the heart. Some of it had pooled up to the gold ornament on his ear.

"No, End, no!" I lifted his large body the best I could, heaving him onto my lap. Red blood covered my hands.

I was so sure we had won. Like a mocking gesture, the last whisps of darkness evaporated from his cooling skin. I waved them ferociously away.

I dimly realized that Calyse and Lizzie had both followed me and stood watching, dark and light, just outside the circle of red leaves.

"We wrote a different ending," I said through my weeping. "You deserve a different ending." I embraced him across the shoulders, laying my cheek against his. He had done this for his kingdom and for me, so I wouldn't meet the same fate as his former love. He had done this to destroy the Shadow.

I hated the Shadow more than I had ever hated anything in this world.

"Our souls are one, remember? Your body and mind you gave to me. So I will tell you a different story." My frenzied whispering became calm enough that I could continue, speaking quickly on each exhale. "Once upon a time, there lived a mortal girl and a Fae king. In the beginning, the girl thought he was wicked, and later on she thought he was wicked, but in between, she fell in love with him."

My voice broke. I felt wrapped in sacrifices—Endymion,

Lizzie's engagement, even Calyse's vow. Was it ever enough? Or would more have to pour themselves out in a futile battle against ruin?

"Shadows filled the Fae King's soul, and she would kiss them out one by one. It seemed there would be no end, until a prophecy foretold their victory against the evil that plagued him. It said, *If she would wed the King, all war against the Enemy will cease and the Enemy alone will be destroyed. The King's mortal bride shall outlive all her kind and remain the fascination of her husband always.*" I gave a sardonic little laugh even as I traced the place where I'd painted those words on his bloodied torso. "And they believed the words. They gave themselves fully to one another and the shadows were defeated. They lived, wild and free, the King and Queen of the Fae. And she loved him."

By the time I spoke the final words of the story, I was whispering into his ear. I remained there when a new idea entered my mind. "Take from me anything you must to give him life. The King belongs to me and I to him."

With a final, brutal curse against the Enemy, I pressed my lips against Endymion's. They were cooling. I breathed into his mouth and sucked the air in again.

I heard a sniff behind me. Calyse. In my peripheral vision, his hand stretched out, but he lowered it again. Good. He wasn't trying to stop me.

"You can't be dead," I told Endymion, kissing him again. "You can't be dead! I vow with blood and mind and bone my troth to thee..." I began reciting in Fae the vows I'd made only hours ago.

I was shaking.

"Please, come away, my queen."

I wrenched my shoulder from Calyse's grasp. He grieved for his friend too, but he'd still been willing to follow out this barbaric order. Now wasn't the time for me to sort out blame, but to reverse what had happened.

"I pledge, come hell or heaven…"

My shaking increased. My eyes and face burned. Everything burned. My trembling became convulsions.

"Laura!" Lizzie cried weakly, crouching to hold me. Her stick-thin arms could do nothing against the racking of my limbs.

Inside and sizzling against my skin, piercing heat raged. I had no choice but to release Endymion. He slumped off my thighs where I'd held him.

Tears streaming now, I arched to the ground, shaking uncontrollably. My eyes, my hands, everything hurt.

I screamed.

A wave of blindness threatened to take me. I tried to fight, releasing another shriek, but it did no good. Perhaps it was shadows or grief or death itself. I didn't know. But it took me.

✣ 31 ✣

I woke, confused, on a rocking ship. Or perhaps not. A hammock?

I couldn't open my eyes. The pain was too great. But I could flex my sticky fingers—why were they sticky?

My head throbbed, but I felt secure, despite the movement all around me, like I wasn't going to fall. Finally, pieces started collecting into sensible shapes in my mind.

Endymion lying dead.

Lizzie and the other maidens wandering out from their enchanted sleep.

Calyse saying he needed to announce me as queen even though he had just killed his best friend.

The searing pain as I held the body of the King.

I wished for unconsciousness again. The rocking slowed to a stop and my back, covered in a black silk cape, lowered into something soft. Everything felt so unreal that I thought I might keep going, sucked down into the softness like being swallowed by wool. Next, my legs and head met the luxurious cushion. A large hand was laid palm down on my stomach. I pushed it up lightly with my breathing, past caring.

"Little thorn." Warmth bathed my ear with the words.

I opened my mouth, pulse spiking, and struggled to open my eyes.

I heard a sigh, then, "Is she...?" The new voice belonged to Calyse.

"Laura, can you hear us?" Lizzie, though her voice sounded unnaturally weak, almost empty.

I raised my hand weakly to force my eyes open. They burned as though I'd swum a long time underwater without closing them. But I could finally see, albeit hazily.

Above me stood a pale, bloody, grand, alive Endymion. He smiled wide, a grin full of teeth.

"Oh, Laura!" Lizzie's face had finally gained a modicum of color. She gripped my hand where it lay on the blue coverlets.

"Don't touch her!" End snapped.

"It's fine," I managed, trying to squeeze my sister's fingers but my muscles had gone weak and my skin was hyper-sensitive.

"Your eyes..." He traced my browbone gently with a fingertip while he drew a blanket up over me. "What did you do?"

"They're gold," Lizzie explained.

I couldn't remember what had happened. Would my pairing with End have transferred the gold in his eyes to me?

"Yours too," I said. The two of us were a fine pair, both so disoriented we could barely speak. And I was so glad everyone I thought was gone stood in this room with me. "What does that mean?"

"It means," said Endymion, brow creased with concern, "you can't cross the barrier."

I blinked. I could never go back to Selene? I could never see my family again? "Is that…?" I looked meaningfully at Lizzie, who shared the same change.

End nodded. I released a shaky breath. Never had I put together that the Fae's unusual glowing eyes meant they couldn't cross into the human lands.

To save him, the sacrifice was worth it, especially since I still had my sister with me. For her, this had to be even more devastating.

Away from our little group, Calyse shifted. End noticed immediately. Cal straightened, lifting his chin in stout obedience to his king.

"You loyal bastard, Cal," the King chuckled, face drawn and intense, but absent of malice. He held out an arm and Calyse clasped it gratefully, brothers again. "Fetch help for the maidens. See that they're taken care of. And leave us alone."

"Sleep short and live long," Calyse replied with a smile.

"You go with him too," I told Lizzie, untangling my fingers from hers. "He'll get you food and water. The food is good here," I added.

When Lizzie looked dubiously at the blood-soaked figures of Endymion and Calyse, I nodded encouragement. I wanted the old Lizzie back, the adventurous, impulsive, romantic, inspiring Lizzie. It would be a long road to get there.

After the two of them left, Endymion and I were alone. I had so many thoughts that for a while I couldn't speak.

"You knew you would go through with it the whole time, didn't you?" My anger surprised me.

"I had no choice. I held off the shadows as long as I could, but by the time Calyse came down, he had to fight them off just to reach me." A haunted expression passed his face and his hand drifted up to where his chest had been slashed. "I hoped you would forgive me and rule in my stead."

"And if I didn't?"

"A queen rageful against the Shadow would be just as effective, if more ruthless." He looked knowingly at me.

I still felt strange, as though I dwelt in a new body—mine and not mine. My eyes weren't the only parts that burned. As my mind and vision cleared, I noticed details far away clearer than they had looked before. The smoky smell of the fire and the smooth scent of the churning pool mingled sharply in the air. Each thread of the blanket slid individually across my skin. I was part of this room as I had never been.

I focused once more on Endymion. "I'm still rageful."

"Reckless, too. A little wicked, even." He smelled like blood and soil.

"Kiss me," I murmured, wanting to taste him before the scent went away. Perhaps he was right.

He obliged, tenderly, barely grazing my lips. I felt each sensation acutely. Oddly, I felt powerful lying there, as though I could will the room warm or the water cool.

Using a knitted piece of clothing dipped in the pool, he sponged me clean of blood. Afterward, I felt strong enough to stand, so I ordered him to disrobe too for me to do the same. Endymion lay on the other side of bed, his gory clothes lying in a pile beside him. There was still a nasty wound above his heart, near the golden words I'd written. Perhaps they'd come true after all. The only article we wore were the matching golden cuffs in our ears.

"I'm sorry you felt you had to save me," he said once I was done. "My death should have necessitated no further sacrifice."

"I will always save you."

He fixed me with a look so honest I nearly quailed. In it, I saw years of pain, of loneliness, of the certainty it wouldn't end like this. "And I would have no one else by my side."

Gently, gently, I kissed him. Exhausted, I crawled back in bed and, together, we fell asleep.

◈

THE NEXT MORNING, MORE COMMOTION FILLED THE DINING room than I'd ever seen. Besides Endymion and I, Calyse, Lizzie, Ellis, dozens of the other captured maidens, attendants, and several of Endymion's Fae warriors all crowded around the long table. Many had to stand along the walls.

A yellow-eyed maiden with partially decayed skin devoured half a melon with ravenous hunger. Lizzie sat beside me, per my request. Her gaze roamed along the table's offerings, snagging on all the sumptuous fruit there. She seemed livelier today than yesterday, but she certainly wasn't herself yet. If another melon had been within her arm's reach, I thought she would have gobbled it whole.

Endymion brooded beside me. At our engagement party he didn't appear to mind the crowds, but he was a fundamentally solitary creature. All this hubbub annoyed him, especially since the clamor of the crowd pulsed with the question, "What next?"

With an infinitely cultured air, he took a measured sip of tea spiked with brandy. Even with everything going on around us, I could smell it.

He set down the teacup with freshly ringed hands. "Silence," he said, not loudly.

The warriors heard and obeyed. Ellis, true to form, hadn't been speaking anyway. The maidens weren't sure what had caused the hush. A few asked their neighbors in an undertone what was happening. I hated how they all looked and acted like subjects of a mad hospital. Hopefully, we could help restore them to whatever they would have been without the fairy fruit.

Endymion whispered something and gestured faintly with his fingers. The candlelight all spontaneously blew out, then reignited. Someone screamed.

"For now, the maidens may have the East Wing. Escort them there. See they are provided for. And bring everyone else to the throne room." He stood suddenly, took my hand, and we exited. I cast a look at Lizzie being herded with the other maidens and made a silent promise to do all I could for her.

"Insufferable," End muttered.

"They don't know what you've been through."

"And we won't tell them."

I stopped. "What?"

Endymion rounded to face me. "I have no intention of telling anyone I was possessed by Im Scathail all this time. You, Calyse, two other warriors, and my mother are the only ones who know the true purpose of my travels, and you are the only ones who know that that purpose has been served. A large cloud was seen last night above the skylights. I will tell them the truth that the Shadow was defeated outside their very doors. By you."

"They'll never believe it," I scoffed. "I'm a human."

We looked at each other. How had we gotten our ending? Calyse had killed the Shadow inside Endymion, but how had I brought him back? The only consequence I could see was that I couldn't pass the barrier, a tiny piece of what it meant to be one of the Fae. Was our soul tie strong enough on its own to resurrect him?

Although I wanted to believe it, part of me couldn't imagine that after hundreds of years, the Enemy would require so small a sacrifice to bring his prize back. Perhaps Im Scathail truly had no more sway, every bit of him encased in Endymion's flesh until it was ripped away.

"They believe what I tell them," End said. His prickly manner softened as he approached me. "If I say that I have chosen for my bride a ferocious warrior among her kind, with words that drip like honey syrup, and a wrath to crush all who displease her, they will believe me."

I stifled a laugh as he bent to kiss my neck. "Such terrible lies."

"Are they?"

I let the question circle in my brain as he did his work. Perhaps they weren't lies at all, just truth seen through a glass.

"I could take you here, you know," he murmured against my shoulder.

We stood in the middle of a lit hallway. Anyone could come through. I did feel much better than last night. My eyes barely stung and my skin was sensitive, but in the most delicious way.

With a dry mouth, I said, "Out in the open?"

"I am King of the Fae. I'm prone to dissipation and excess..." He drew a line sweeping up the side of my neck with his tongue.

I moaned.

He hiked me up so he could hold me with my legs around his waist.

"We have to announce ourselves," I gasped. "And we have to tell your kingdom the Enemy has been defeated."

After one more firm kiss in which I could taste his disappointment, he set me down. Every point of contact felt alive.

"Yes, I can take you in the throne room instead."

At my astonished expression, he laughed and walked away.

I HAD NEVER BEEN TO THE THRONE ROOM BEFORE. I PICTURED the place where Endymion and I had sat during the betrothal celebration, but this was different. As far as I could reckon, the throne room lay in the same area of the castle as the King's bedchamber. It looked quite unlike not only the King's room, but any other space I'd ever laid eyes on.

The room formed a semicircle like our little outdoor theatre back in Selene. The curving walls held painted frescos mirroring scenes of the forest surrounding the castle, as well as birds, beasts, forest creatures, and Fae in every attitude of war or repose.

All focus immediately drew away from those walls, however, to settle on the throne in the center. A wolf, of all things, lounged beside it, unchained. I was glad to see it had yellow eyes. The back of the throne itself rose up and fanned out like a bird's tail of enormous proportions. Gnarled dark wood formed the magnificent chair, shaped so cunningly that it seemed to be one piece. Embedded in the wood were veins of gold and rose-hued precious stones.

It was a wonder to behold, but the most unusual feature of the room was the water. A skimming of water began over the frescos, then swished over the floor toward the royal throne, wolf and all, ending just shy of the throne's feet where it washed into a miniature moat. Lily pads floated on the surface of the thin pond.

Endymion and I waded through the layer of water between standing rows of forest creatures and animals until we stepped over the water to the other side. The great wolf didn't stir except to acknowledge the King's presence.

Before End even made his announcement, many obviously noticed my golden ear cuff that was the twin to the King's. A few in the front row preemptively shuffled to one knee, despite getting wet.

"The Shadow," he said, "is gone."

At first there was no sound but the trickle of water. The edges of the room undulated with patterns of light. It was as though a collective gasp had sucked all air from the room.

"We have defeated it," I added, nervous about speaking to so many at once. Scarred faces stared at me with disconcerting focus.

A murmur. A cry.

"*She* has defeated it. All hail your Queen!"

The rest dropped to a knee. I even saw little Zuca's sour face among them. A rhythmic splashing rose. Hands, staffs, and feet beat against the water. The result was an ethereal, savage heartbeat. I almost wondered if they were all connected.

With a shout from Endymion, they ceased, rose, and cheered. Noise echoed off the walls. The wolf narrowed its eyes but remained lying by the arm of the throne. Everything felt like a dream.

End led me to the throne now, inviting me to sit with him as we had done at the party. His lips had a roguish tilt. I couldn't help picturing what it would be like for him to press his hard body over me against this throne, and for everyone to see him drive into me.

I shook myself. His presence made me imagine unholy things. He caught my blush, if the mirth in his eye was any indication.

Once the cheering died down, End took on an insolent air. It amazed me how quickly he could switch from being brooding and authoritative to teasingly wicked. "I will tell you a story, if my queen will permit me," he said expansively.

I cocked my jaw, wondering what he was up to, but nodded for him to continue.

"Once on the time, there was a Fae king and a mortal girl..."

He got all the phrases wrong, all the story mixed up, and I thought at one point that no one in the audience understood this as invention rather than fact. His version painted the mortal girl as the most fearsome in the land and the Fae king as the most dreadful. Their love conquered all darkness, though the tale bore little resemblance to its source.

I was charmed. Some clapped uncertainly at the end.

Why were their reactions so lackluster? It wasn't the best story, but it was one of the first he'd ever told, and he was their king.

I raised a hand to his cheek to give him a kiss.

We both saw it at the same time.

From my hands rose twisting dark shadows.

$$\text{32}$$

"Get out!" cried the King, enraged and clearly frightened. "Get out!"

All the lights in the throne room extinguished, plunging us in darkness. Only the faintest glimmers in the water reflected back to us.

Screams and splashing echoed off the walls, hurting my heightened senses. Under me, Endymion moved, setting me on my feet. I clasped my hands together as though I could feel the shadows unfurling from them. They didn't feel any different than they had since saving End.

The commotion gradually lessened as the Fae, the forest creatures, and everyone else retreated from the volatile throne room. With the noise reduced, I now heard a rolling growl.

"End, please, the lights!" I said, gazing into the darkness in vain. Where was the wolf?

He grabbed my arm and pulled me behind the massive wooden throne so no onlookers could see us.

Sight returned in a flash and a flutter of his fingers. He gazed at my hands with the eyes of a haunted man. There was still the suggestion of writhing darkness around my fingers, in my palm.

"What did you do?" he hissed, utterly breathless.

"I don't—"

The wolf stalked around the side of the throne toward us, hackles raised. Its yellow eyes glared at me as surely as if it had been bred to hunt the Shadow no matter what form it took.

I shrank back. The beast's back, now that it was standing, rose as high as my chest. The very air seemed to vibrate from its low growl.

End said something in Fae. The wolf didn't respond to the command, if it had been a command. He pushed me partially behind him, shielding me with his body.

It was as if Endymion weren't there at all. The wolf's attention never left me. Its path curved to bypass the obstacle that was the Fae King, every step deliberate, coiled.

We couldn't run. Unless End could simply disappear and appear in a new place, pass through walls, we couldn't outrun this creature.

Snarling, it sprang.

I screamed and held my hands out in self-protection. What happened next shocked me to my very bones.

From my palms shot a stream of dark smoke that toppled the beast while it was still in mid-air. The wolf tumbled away from us, skidding almost to the far wall.

Too shocked to make sense of what had happened, I seized Endymion's hand and we sprinted for the nearest door, a back exit I hoped would take us away from where the crowd had gone. He wrenched the door open and slammed it shut behind us.

Panting, I leaned against the wall, gazing down uncomprehendingly at my own hands. Using only force of will, I could amplify or reduce the flickering darkness. I tried to make all trace of shadow disappear. After a few tries, I managed to do it.

Only then did I meet Endymion's narrowed gaze. "How?" His tone sounded much like the wolf's growl.

"I don't know. Have you ever done that?"

"No."

I thought of him stumbling through the corridor, panic in his eyes as the shadows overtook him and hunted me. But now I didn't feel hunted or possessed.

I felt... powerful.

"What did you give in exchange for me, little thorn?" he asked, expression drawn and desolate.

I wanted to comfort him, but knew somehow that he would shy away from my touch. "I offered everything," I answered truthfully.

"He was defeated." His chest was heaving now. "With my death, he was defeated. You had no right to undo that."

"I didn't."

He glared at my shadowless hands, jaw flexing. His voice became empty. "We must test you. I hope you're right. I will not survive if you are wrong. A third death will be my last."

Rose. He was talking about Rose, then his sacrifice the other day, and now... Would I have to be sacrificed too for us to truly be rid of this menace? My blood chilled.

Summoning my nerve, I straightened. "I believe he is still defeated," I said. "The Shadow is not controlling me." I opened my palm once more. Darkness curled there like a cloudy storm. Simply by making a fist, I shut it off. "I control it. I am its master now."

His brow furrowed. "Let us hope so."

Endymion's eyes were blank, the golden fire all but extinguished. We had returned to the lower floor. Calyse was there with my sister. He seemed to have taken his charge to watch after her quite literally. I didn't think she needed to be here to see this.

"One day," said Calyse, "you'll have to choose someone else to do this for you. I'm retiring and will only come out for revels or performances." His half-hearted joke earned no smiles.

I sat in the moss-green armchair in the little library. End had muttered something about how I would be more comfortable there. He had never told me what test was performed to see if the shadows were still in him.

With a knife in one hand and a small cup in the other, Calyse sliced his finger and let three drops of blood fall into the liquid. He swirled them around, speaking to the potion in Fae, before handing it over to me. Calyse stood battle ready. I looked uncertainly from him to Lizzie, who blinked in confusion, to Endymion, whose carved features had become a mask.

"This will determine the truth," he said.

"It can take a few hours," Calyse added, though his stance suggested that I could explode right there.

I thought of how many times Endymion had done this very thing, hopeful at first and then gradually more and more despairing. Had Calyse been there through it all? They both looked weary and sad with repetition.

I inhaled slowly, trying to steel myself before downing the bitter liquid in the cup.

A cough exploded from me. The potion burned. I pictured my insides corroding like fire eating through paper. My fingers dug into the fabric armrests of the chair as I writhed in pain.

Then, just as quickly as the fiery sensation spread, it petered out, tingling along my extremities. Hauling in breath, I looked at my body. No shadows.

When it was clear nothing more would happen, Calyse said, "We'll know for sure in a few hours. If nothing happens by tomorrow, we'll have our answer." He glanced at Endymion, who still stood there, stoic. "I've never heard of someone commanding shadows, but it would be better than the alternative. Right, End?"

"It would."

Calyse looked reassuringly at Lizzie, who gazed at me with abstracted concern. "Will she be all right?" she asked.

"Hopefully," Cal answered before turning back to me. "A few hours, then. We'll meet right here."

The tension in the room had reduced somewhat after the burning potion hadn't caused smoky darkness to billow out of me, but I still felt the thick uncertainty in the air. I decided not to try out my new ability until those few hours had passed. Until then, I would make sure there were no unintentional shadows that could make Endymion misinterpret the results of this test.

Back to my bedroom, then. It felt as though I was always being hidden away in that room. Without a word, I stood, oddly ashamed.

Calyse left with Lizzie.

Endymion's sharp edges relaxed. "I'm sorry," he said.

"For what?"

"For imposing my hell on you. I assure you my life was not worth it. Come." He took my hand, first touching it as though it were hot as burning metal and then lacing our fingers together once he found no danger. He tugged me toward the door. "We'll reassure them all that there is no threat, and then we will make it so."

Together, instead of returning to my room, we ascended the stairs and walked across the huge arcade all the way to the King's bedchamber. Eyes followed us—more, I assumed, than would normally have done so by virtue of being royalty. The awe that surrounded Endymion had become a new level of fear. Everyone made a wide way for us. He didn't look at any of them.

He pulled open the wide doors depicting peace and war.

"How long do we have to wait?" I asked. At first, I had been fairly sure that I controlled these new shadows. Now, I feared I was wrong. And what would happen if I was?

"To be safe?" Endymion rubbed the back of his neck. "Tomorrow morning. The Enemy enjoys attacking in the dead of night." He said it bitterly.

"Aren't you afraid, then? I should be alone."

"I am afraid," he admitted, facing me. "But you should never be alone. I judged the situation hastily." He stood close, towering above me. "The way I see it, either you're right and there is no danger, which makes you the most powerful Fae queen in memory, or you're wrong, and I will survive that no better than you will. No matter what outcome, we will face it together."

Relief flooded my body. I hadn't realized how much End's distant behavior weighed on me. I held back tears as I embraced him.

He sighed. "This night calls for wine."

Luckily for both of us, there was plenty sitting on a sideboard in pitchers and bottles and goblets. We brought a tray to the bed on the dais, parting the gauzy curtains to cocoon ourselves inside. Soon we were naked, drinking wine from each other's mouths and pouring it over our chests with the abandon of a last day alive. We grunted and strained and thrust into each other in a wild haze. Endymion found a crown and placed it on my head. I commanded; he obeyed. He commanded; I obeyed.

When we came to, we were laced with delicious red marks and

the stickiness of licked-off wine. I clung to him, leg thrown over his hip, as if he could save me from drowning.

33

No shadows erupted from me that afternoon, that night, or that morning.

I sat up in bed and smiled at Endymion. "See?" I said, though I could hardly believe it myself.

"My fearsome queen," he growled and pulled me down for a kiss. When we pulled apart, he asked, "Can you still command them?"

I opened my hand face up, willing darkness to appear there. It did, licking up toward the ceiling like flame.

The King watched in wonder. Tentatively, he tapped each of my callused fingertips, then swiped his finger over the shadow.

"What does it feel like?" I asked. To me, it felt a bit like water in my hand.

"Pressure, like wind, but no pain." Staring at the darkness, he gave it a creative curse, then smirked at me. "What else can you do with it?"

I directed my palm at the gauzy drapes around the bed. A stream of shadows blew the curtains aside.

"What else?"

I placed both palms together, then drew them apart. A roiling ball of darkness churned in my hands. I blasted it against a bare space on the wall. The shadows burst and unfurled, lingering a moment before disappearing again.

"What else?"

I could tell from his breathless tone and hooded eyes how aroused he was. I gently directed one of the shadows to his hair, rubbing along his scalp and curling around his neck. He let his head tip back, eyes closed, mouth open.

Not long after, we emerged, both washed and crowned, from the bedchamber. Endymion called for Calyse. He found us under the domed skylight. Because of the sensitive nature of the experiment, he merely raised one black eyebrow.

"Nothing," End announced.

Calyse's orange eyes brightened. "Nothing?"

"Nothing," I confirmed. "I control them completely."

Endymion cast me a sultry look, unbefitting human royalty but at home in untamed world of the Fae.

Calyse laughed, hearty and loud. He embraced the King and pounded his chest in salute of me.

"Already composing a victory song?" Endymion teased.

"I've had one waiting for decades," Cal shot back.

"Where's Lizzie?" I asked.

Cal's jubilant expression lost its edge. "I left her with the other maidens. She comes and goes." I understood he meant her mind.

I nodded, solemn. Once she was restored, there would be even more cause for celebration.

Another thought pinged in my chest. I turned to End. "There's one more thing I want to do."

I STOOD WHERE THE BARRIER LAY CLOSEST TO MY HOUSE. I couldn't quite see it through the trees. When I inched forward, the toes of my shoes pressed upward as though encountering a pane of glass.

Lizzie stood beside me. I held her hand as I set the note atop a small heap of golden riches.

Dear Mother, Grandmother, and Great-grandmother, it read, *Lizzie and I are alive. Please don't mourn for us. We live now in the castle of the Fae King, who treats us well. We have everything we need but your companionship. Please accept this gift for all the love you've shown us. You may expect more every year at this time. If you wait for us here next year, perhaps we can speak face to face, and I can tell you all that happened. To write it in a letter is impossible—it would sound too sensational. We love you, but we may not cross the barrier. With all my love, Laura*

"They'll be all right," I told Lizzie with a lump in my throat. I knew my place in the Fae court now. Lizzie just needed to find hers. I hugged her sideways.

Together, we lingered a little longer, hoping to catch a glimpse of the rest of our family. Of course, they didn't appear. The barrier wasn't deep in the forest, but it cut through out of sight of the village, and none of them would venture that far.

Finally, we turned back. Endymion and Calyse waited on their steeds for us.

"*Dear, you should not stay so late,*" I sang in Lizzie's ear as we approached.

"*Twilight is not good for maidens,*" she chimed in, some of the old light dancing in her eyes, though there was sadness too.

We sang the last part together merrily as we mounted the horses.

"*Should not loiter in the glen*
In the haunts of goblin men."

Lizzie wants only two things: fairy fruit and freedom. Standing in her way is the Fae King's best friend, a rugged but altogether too jovial warrior named Calyse.

Trapped in the Fae kingdom after waking from enchanted sleep, Lizzie misses the independence she once enjoyed. Calyse, assigned to oversee her recovery, watches her every move. Their forced proximity nearly drives her mad, and even grates on Calyse, who used to aid the King himself, though it's hard to tell between the wicked smiles and dirty banter.

Even though they're at odds, Lizzie and Calyse agree that acting on their undeniable attraction could distract each other from their problems. But even their rough, blazing encounters can't fix her broken pieces until, after a terrible evil threatens the castle, she discovers there's more to their connection than she thought.

y benchmate had brown hair, long and scraggly, and one of her pale eyelids looked swollen.

"I'm Lizzie. I'm from Selene, like you are, right?"

She turned her slow, dazed attention to me. "Selene, yes."

My attempt at a smile turned real. "Do you know the cottage closest to the woods? That's where I live. Lived."

"With the old women?"

My family was the only one in Selene made up entirely of women—four generations packed together inside that little cottage. In a village known for its maidens going missing, envy followed us and suitors followed me. I could tell her association with the house wasn't positive.

"Yes," I confirmed.

She took another deliberate sip of soup.

"And you are?"

"I?" She wavered, almost as if she couldn't remember. "I am Georgina."

Her name sounded somewhat familiar. She must have disappeared when I was only a child, but the names of those who had heeded the call of the forest echoed in the village for years afterward.

"Perhaps we could go for a walk some evening," I said, cheered by my own private defiance. Calyse didn't like that I walked at night to clear my mind. Well, then I could do it with someone else with whom I had more in common.

Georgina chewed her lip meditatively for a while. Her eyes had gone absent again. They glowed low like embers. "Do you know where we... could go?"

I understood her question perfectly. Fairy fruit. It was never far from any of our minds. I decided I wouldn't tell her it was all gone from the castle. "I thought just a walk to get some exercise, maybe talk for a bit."

Her swollen eye twitched with disappointment, but she sucked in a breath and answered, "Let's."

I patted her arm encouragingly, then turned back to my own soup. I could still help someone.

"Oh good. I stepped away and thought you might have fled for an exit," said Calyse, settling down next to me and pulling a large, vegetable-studded ham toward himself.

It wasn't rare for him to stop in to see how I was doing, but the other women had begun to notice his incessant hovering. It was embarrassing.

"Not before soup," I said archly. I flourished my spoon. *See, I'm eating.*

He smiled, though I'm sure he could tell his presence didn't delight me. Besides his rankling surveillance, I also hated the zing that crackled through my skin in the innocent places we touched. The bench was small for his big body, so his thigh rested against mine. So did his massive arm. I felt dwarfed and conspicuous. Other beings could elicit this response from me—not my jailer.

He took massive bites of the meat. I curled my lip in disgust.

Finally, he caught my look. "Still judging me for my diet, are you? How do you think I became like this?" He flexed his arm to demonstrate. The muscles were undeniably... impressive.

I blinked. "Being born Fae I thought was enough," I replied.

"It helps." He shoved more ham into his mouth. "I really am curious how you humans operate on so little. Or is it only you maidens?"

I disliked the term. "We were asleep for months or even years, so I don't think we are the best examples of humans as a whole."

He tipped his mouth. "Sounds fair."

When he finished his meal and we moved away from the table so as not to be overheard, I said in an undertone, "I think I would like to hit you again today."

"You're not sore from last time?" His eyes sparkled with a little too much mirth.

I was sore. My shoulders and biceps and sides ached, but that did nothing to lessen my resolve. "No."

His expression mocked my lie. "If that's what you want, we can go back."

"And I'm planning to take a walk this evening with a friend."

His brows rose. "A friend? You found someone you can stand to be with?"

Unexpectedly, the comment stung. "Yes. Georgina. She was sitting on the other side of me. She needs a friend and I would like to know her better. Will that suit?"

He shrugged. "I have no order but to stare at your face whenever you choose to emerge, so that doesn't bother me," he said lightly.

The reminder did nothing to alleviate my mood. "Can I hit you now?"

He chuckled. "You can try."

☙❧

I did try.

I let my swirling pain rise like oil to the surface as I lashed out, but just like last time, Calyse's defensive moves foiled every attempt I made to get near him.

The main part of the training area actually had running drills in it, so we moved to a smaller adjacent room intended for this kind of sparring. The floors felt spongier and the walls were draped with golden Fae heraldry.

"I like your spirit," he said, barely winded.

I, on the other hand, streamed with sweat and couldn't have spoken if I wanted to. If my sore muscles had ripped, I hardly would have been in more pain.

Finally, I halted my attack, trying to catch my breath. In an odd way, the pain felt good. Yes, my face no doubt looked as red as a poisonous mushroom and furious tears masqueraded as sweat down my face, but it felt good nonetheless. It was pain I could understand.

"Is that enough?" he asked, planting the stave next to him like a traveler's staff.

I shook my head and lifted the rod once more. Hot pain seared through my side. I twisted sideways to combat the sting but it only lanced deeper. Dropping the stave, I winced.

Calyse was with me in an instant. "Not to worry," he said, his low voice practiced and soothing. I wondered how many times he had done this. "Just lie down. Bring your knees together, like that."

I grimaced as I lowered myself to the ground and rolled to my back. He crouched beside me and gently held the side of my knees, laying them down to one side. The knifing pain shot through me again.

"It's all right. It's all right. Just a sprain, it looks like. Not even a very bad one." He held my knees down and placed his other hand on my shoulder to keep me from rotating with my legs.

Once I was able to take a few deep breaths, he smirked at me. "I knew you were lying earlier. This is a lot of exertion if you're not used to it."

"I'm strong enough. I just..." But I didn't know what to say.

"Now I want you to roll onto your stomach."

Straightening my knees painfully, I did as he said.

Strong fingers explored my shoulders, massaging the muscle,

and rotating my arms. His expert hands gave just the right pressure, knew where to go to address that sweet ache from the fight. My pulse beat harder everywhere. I didn't want him to stop. He dug into the muscle just behind my shoulder and I had to hold in an unseemly noise. He concentrated there for a while before moving my arm in precise ways, finally bringing both arms, fully extended, above my head. It was a worshipful position, full of abandon.

While I stretched out, his hands moved down to explore my side. I flinched when he began kneading my waist.

"Does that hurt?" he murmured.

"Not enough."

"You say such naughty things."

If he was trying to scandalize me again, it wasn't working. Seducing would be a better word. Surely, by now he could feel the pound of my heartbeat, the shallowness of my breath.

After all, was it so bad to want Calyse? In other moments, I could still despise him for keeping me under guard. For now, I longed for him to touch me everywhere.

I held still under his hands. At least I had this...

No. I wanted more. I'd let him know I wanted more.

Releasing a satisfied moan, I reached back for his arm. Immediately, he stopped massaging me.

Heart thundering, I sat up. The ache in my side had dwindled to a pleasant soreness.

Did his flirtations mean nothing after all? Had I just made a fool of myself?

On his knees, he eyed me warily, the ghost of a hesitant smile on his lips. "Well, you are an enigma. If you're trying to make me spend less time with you, that sound wasn't the way." His voice and chuckle were both husky.

Slowly, in case I was wrong, I crawled closer. He watched me hungrily as I propped myself up in front of him.

He narrowed his eyes roguishly. "I'm sorry, do you hate me or want me?"

"Both, sometimes," I admitted. "Is this all right?"

"If the lady wants."

When I leaned in against his broad chest, muscles clearly delineated even through the leather armor, he held me gently but firmly in place. His hand took up a good portion of my back.

His amber and smoke scent filled my lungs as I brought my face to his. His kiss made my body alight as if I felt him everywhere. His lips moved as his fingers had, searching, knowing just the right moment to dig in for more.

I moaned and settled even closer, straddling his lap. I felt him smile against my mouth. His lips opened under mine, inviting and erotic. I licked inside, and I felt the hard bulge of his trousers between my legs. Bold, I rocked against him, hanging onto his strong back as I ground hard against his erection. The motion teased my ache, raised my pulse.

Calyse's arms felt like rock, unmoving, as though he feared that if he submitted to this growing pleasure he would crush me. Finally, he raised one upward and wrapped my braid around one fist, tugging my head back.

I released a cry. I didn't slow the rolling of my hips as he bent to kiss my neck. Kissing became biting when I bucked right over the spot where I was wettest. He groaned, holding the very place by my neck where his fingers had massaged but this time with his teeth.

"Yes," I said, letting him know I enjoyed this. He wasn't hurting me. To punctuate my word, I thrust hard against him.

I earned a loud groan and an extra tug on my braid. His tongue traced a path along the bitemarks and up to the soft spot beneath my chin. Now he was thrusting back up into me, little movements, almost involuntary. I gasped as he hit my pulsing ache just right.

With a feral growl, he swept me to the floor, his huge body on top of me. He kept his weight off me except for where he crushed me with his lips and thrust hard and insistent between my legs. I kept them spread, inviting more pressure to fill my pulsing need. My wet undergarments were surely soiling his armor from such firm, demanding rubbing.

After a few more minutes, Calyse let out a mighty groan and I knew it was over. He brought his lips to mine one more time, then rolled to lay beside me.

Still breathing heavily, he grinned at me, shaking his head. "I didn't expect *that* to happen today," he said.

"And we still have our clothes on." I felt bleary and achy and very good.

He laughed. "Imagine if we hadn't."

I already was. "Calyse." I didn't know when this idea had started, but now that it was here, it didn't feel new. "I enjoyed that."

"Naturally."

"Don't ruin it. I was thinking, what if we..." An odd shyness crept up on me. Laura was the shy one, not me. "What if we... helped each other? I need a distraction and you"—I eyed his full lips, the muscles in his torso—"you are a very good distraction. As aggravating as you can be, we both... need someone. Not forever. But for now."

"Are you asking me for regular sex?"

I scrunched my face. "Yes."

"Well..." He placed one hand behind his head and looked wistfully at the ceiling. "I'm not opposed to a little excitement." He sighed. "You have more fire in you than I thought, human girl."

"Just call me Lizzie."

"Not my sweet nemesis?"

"Lizzie's fine."

"I like nemesis too."

READ TRAPPED BY THE FAE NOW!

READ MORE BY ZORA FOX

Fae and Shadow duology
End of the Forest
Trapped by the Fae

Deathless Love—novels
Wings and Blindness
Flowers and the Far Realm
Flame and Warpaint
Temptation and Tridents

Deathless Love—novellas
Storm and Sanctuary
Full Moons and Vampires
Candle Wax and Sunlight

Deathless Love—short stories
Lovers and Monsters
Secrets and Midnights

Join the Foxy newsletter and read Wings and Blindness FREE!

What if Psyche was sent to kill Eros from the beginning?

When Psyche is thrown out of the temple into dangerous streets, Queen Cytherea makes her an offer. Kill Eros, and earn the goddess' favor.

Disguised as a creature to avoid assassination, Eros has long been the goddess' target. Even lovers have betrayed him because of her. After years of lonely nights, he determines to fight back, but his allies will only help if he agrees to marry someone powerless. A human.

When the monster of the mountains demands women for his bride, Psyche has the perfect opportunity to discover if the monster is really Eros in hiding. Seducing the demi-god of passion is a challenge, though, because he doesn't allow himself to be seen or touched. To get him alone, she'll have to bed him as his wife.

This first book in the Deathless Love series welcomes you to the Eight Realms, where danger and desire lurk in every corner, and mythology isn't quite as you remember it.

www.ingramcontent.com/pod-product-compliance
Lightning Source LLC
Chambersburg PA
CBHW021726190726

48289CB00008B/2716